Romain Rolland

Colas Breugnon
A Burgundian Story

Colas Breugnon

A Burgundian Story

by

Romain Rolland

Author of "Jean-Christophe,"
"Mahatma Gandhi," and "Pierre and Luce"

MONDIAL

Mondial
New York

Romain Rolland: Colas Breugnon. A Burgundian Story

Translated by Katherine Miller

French original title:
Colas Breugnon. Récit bourguignon (1919)

Copyright © 2009 Mondial
(for this print edition of "Colas Breugnon")
Editor (2009): Andrew Moore

Cover image: Christophe Finot
("Château-Chinon (Ville), Nievre, Burgundy, France")
(Source: http://fr.wikipedia.org/wiki/Fichier:Panorama_-_Chateau-Chinon_2.jpg)

ISBN 978-1-59569-133-0
Library of Congress Control Number: 2009924956

www.mondialbooks.com

To
Saint Martin of Gaul
Patron Saint of Clamecy

"St. Martin gaily drinks his fill
and lets the stream flow to the mill."
xvi[th] cent. Proverb

Contents

Preface After the War

When the War broke out this book was already printed and ready to appear, so I have left it untouched. The grandchildren of Colas Breugnon have just emerged as heroes and victims of a bloody epic, only to show an unquenchable flame to the world. Let me hope that the people of Europe, full of courage in spite of their sufferings, may find some solace in these reflections of "a little lamb caught between the wolf and the shepherd."

Romain Rolland
November, 1918.

To the Reader

The readers of "Jean-Christophe" certainly never expected this new volume, but they cannot be more surprised than I am myself. I had sketched out other works, — a play and a novel on subjects of the day, in somewhat the same tragic key as "Jean-Christophe," but I had to break off abruptly, throwing aside all my notes and well-planned scenes, for this trifling work which only came into my head the day before. This book is a reaction from the constraint of "Jean-Christophe," which, like an outgrown cuirass, fitted well enough at first, but had become too tight for me; I felt an absolute need of something gay, in the true Gallic spirit—even perhaps verging on impropriety.

On returning to my native place for the first time since my youth, the renewed contact with the soil of Burgundy woke a past within me which I had believed silent forever; and roused all the Colas Breugnons under my skin, so that I was forced to speak for them — as if their tongues had not wagged enough in their lifetime!

They took advantage of the circumstance that one of their descendants chanced to have the pen of a ready writer (something that they had always coveted) and turned me into their secretary. To my protestations, "Now, Grandad, you had your day, it is my turn to speak now," they only answered: "Young one, you can talk when we have finished. In the first place you have nothing more interesting to say, so sit down, and listen with all your ears: you might do that much for the old man; when you stand where I am now you will know that silence is the worst of death."

How could I help writing what was dictated to me? Now it is all over and I am free again—at least I suppose so—and can take up the thread of my own thoughts, if some one of these old chatter-boxes does not take it into his head to start up from the tomb and impart to me his message to posterity.

I am afraid that the society of my Colas Breugnon will not amuse my readers as much as the author; but they must take the book for what it is; something perfectly frank and straightforward which has no idea of transforming or explaining the world either politically, or metaphysically. He is just a true Frenchman, who laughs because he is well and hearty and life is sweet to him.

One cannot escape the Maid of Orleans at the beginning of a French story, so, as she used to say, "Take kindly to it"!

Romain Rolland
May, 1914.

Colas Breugnon

I
The Lark of Candlemas-Day

THANKS be to St. Martin, business is bad, so there is no use in breaking
one's back; and Lord knows I have worked hard enough in my time to
take a little rest and comfort here at my table, with a bottle of wine on my
right hand, the ink-well on the left, and a new quire of paper before me.

"Your good health, old boy!" I say to myself, "I am to have a talk
with you now," Downstairs I can hear my wife raging while the wind
roars outside and I am told there are threatenings of war. Well, let them
be!—How jolly it is to be alone face to face with the best fellow in the
world (I am talking of course of my other self, of you, Colas, with your
old red phiz, and queer grin, with your long Burgundian nose all askew
like a hat on one ear). Tell me if you can why it is so good to see you like
this, just our two selves; to look closely at your elderly countenance,
touching lightly, as it were, on the wrinkles, and to drink a bumper
of old remembrance from the bottom of my heart which is like a deep
well, worse luck! It is pleasant enough to dream, but still better to pin
one's dreams down to paper! However, I am no visionary, but wide-
awake, full of fun and clear-sighted, with no idle fancies in my head.
I only tell what I have seen, done, and said; and for whom do I write?
Certainly not for fame; for I am no fool, and know what I amount to,
the Lord be praised!

I write for my grandchildren? Little will be left of all my scribblings
in ten years, as the old woman is jealous of them, and burns whatever
she can lay hands on. For whom, then? Why, for my other self, of course,
for our good pleasure.—I am sure I should burst if I did not write! Truly
I am not for nothing the child of my grandfather, who could not sleep
unless he had put down on the edge of his pillow the number of flagons
he had emptied. I feel I must talk, and here in Clamecy I have had my
fill of word contests. I must break loose, like the fellow who shaved
King Midas. I know my tongue runs away with me; and it would be
at the risk of my neck if I were heard; but what's the odds! without its
dangers life would be flat enough. I am like our big white oxen, and
love to chew the cud of the day's food. How good it is to taste, feel,
and handle all one has thought, observed, or picked up; to smack one's
lips, to relish, as one tells it over to one's self, something one snapped
up hastily—it seems to melt in one's mouth, and slip down softly; and
how good it is to glance around one's little world and say, "All this is

mine, here I am lord and master, no frost or cold can nip me; here reigns no king, no pope! Not even my old shrew!" But now I must take an account of this world of mine.

The first and best of my possessions is myself. Colas Breugnon, a good Burgundian, plain and straightforward, with a well-rounded waistcoat. I am not exactly in my first youth—fifty last birthday,—but well set-up, my teeth still good, and my sight as clear as a fish's. My beard still sprouts vigorously, but is undoubtedly grayish, and I can't help regretting the fair hair of my youth, and would not say no, if you offered to set my clock back twenty or thirty years. But after all ten lusters are a fine thing. The youngsters may laugh, but how many of them could have paraded up and down France as I have done, for all these years? Lord! how much sun and rain have hit this old back! I have been roasted, soaked, and warmed over dozens of times and my body, like a cracked leather sack, is full of joy and sorrow, spite and good-humor, wisdom and folly, hay and straw, figs and grapes, fruit ripe and unripe, roses and haws—what I have seen, felt and known, owned and lived, all jumbled together in the game-bag, and what fun to dive into it;—but hold on, Colas! We will go into that tomorrow, we shall never be done if we take it up today, so just now we will draw up the inventory of all property belonging to me.

I own a house, a wife, four boys, and a girl (thank God she is married!), eighteen grandchildren, a gray donkey, a dog, six hens, and a pig.—So, I may be called rich. I want to look closely at these treasures, so I must put on my glasses, for, to tell the truth, the latter items exist only in memory. Wars have swept over them, soldiers of the enemy and friends too, so the pig was long ago salted down, the ass foundered, the cellar emptied, and the fowls plucked. I have the wife still, by Heavens! It is not easy to forget my happiness when I hear that squalling tongue,—she's a fine old bird, and mine to the last feather. The whole town envies Breugnon, the old scamp. Come on then, gentlemen, speak up, if you would like to have her! She is a saving, active, sober, good woman, with all the virtues, but they do not seem to fatten her, and I must confess, fellow-sinner, that I like one plump little frailty better than all the seven bony virtues. Well, since it is the will of God, let us be good for lack of something better. Hear her rushing about; her bones seem to be everywhere. She goes poking and climbing, sulking, scolding, grumbling, growling from garret to cellar; dirt and tranquillity flee at her approach. Nearly thirty years ago we were married. Devil take me if I know why! I was smitten with another girl who jilted me, and my wife doted on me because I cared nothing for her. At that time she was small, dark and pale, with hard bright eyes which seemed to eat into me as two drops of acid burn steel; but she loved and *loved* me fit to kill herself! Men are such fools, that by dint of running after me (through pity, vanity too, because I was tired of it all, and because I wanted to get rid of her; a fine way I took to do it!) I became her husband; Johnnie the fool, who kept out of the rain when he jumped in the pool. Ever since, she and all the cardinal virtues dwell in my house, but she would like to get even with me, sweet creature that she is! to make up for the love she threw at me. She wants to stir me up; but it can't be done, I like my ease too much, and I am not such a fool as to make myself unhappy for a word more or less. Let the rain come down, my voice echoes the thunder and I only laugh when she screams. Why shouldn't she scream if she likes it? Why should I keep a woman from such a simple pleasure when I do not want to kill her? Women and silence do not dwell together; so let her sing her song, and I will sing mine. As long as she does not try to shut my mouth (and she will not attempt that, if she is wise) she may warble as she likes, each to his own music.

We may not have been exactly in tune, but none the less we played some pretty pieces together; a girl and four boys, all good and well-built regardless of expense, but of the lot the only one in whom I see my own flesh is my girl, Martine, the little witch! What a time I had with her before I got her safely married! She has settled down now, though I don't count too much on it, but it is no longer my business to look after her and trot about at her heels; my son-in-law can take his turn. She and I always wrangle whenever we meet, but at bottom we understand each other as no one else does; she is a good sort, cautious even when she seems most reckless, good too, if there is fun in it; for boredom is to her worse than wickedness. She does not mind trouble, for that means effort, which is joy, and she loves life and has an eye for what is good. My blood runs in her veins, the only trouble is I gave her too much of it.

The boys are not quite so successful. There was an undue share of the mother in them and the dough did not rise; two out of the four are bigots like her, and what is worse their bigotries are antagonistic, for one is always running after priests' skirts, while the other is a Huguenot. I cannot think how I came to hatch out such a couple of ducks. My third son is a soldier, and has to fight, when he is not loafing about, God knows where! and the fourth is just a nonentity; a little sheepish, insignificant shopkeeper — it makes me yawn to think of him, but when the whole of us are seated round the table, each with a fork in his fist, then I feel indeed that we are all of one breed, all of one mind; and well worth looking at, our jaws going like clockwork, bread and wine disappearing down the trapdoor.

You have heard of the furniture, now let us talk of the house itself, which is like another daughter to me, for I built it with my own hands bit by bit, and some parts over and over again, on the banks of the Beuvron, which flows along slowly smooth and green, full of grass, mud and slime, just where the suburbs begin on the other side of the bridge which is like a crouching hound with the water licking below.

Directly in front the tower of St. Martin rises light and proud, its edges like an embroidered skirt. They tell us the steps leading to Paradise are dark and steep; so are those of Old Rome leading up to the carved doorway. My shell, my niche is outside the walls, and the result of that is that when from the top of St. Martin's tower they spy an enemy in the plain the town shuts its gates, and the enemy comes to me;—I could get along without that sort of visit, though I like conversation as a general thing. So I leave the key under the door, and get out, but when I come back it sometimes happens that both door and key have disappeared, leaving only the four walls, and then I have to rebuild. My friends say to me, "Stupid! to take all this trouble for the enemy. Come out of your mole-hill into the town where you will be safe." But I always answer, "I know when I am well off. Perhaps I should be safer behind a thick wall, but what could I see there? the wall, and nothing else. That would bore me to death, for I need elbow room; and I like to spread myself out along my river bank, and when I am in my little garden, with nothing to do, I love to watch the reflections in the still water, the bubbles the fish make on the surface and the long-tressed weeds stirring at the bottom. I fish there too, or even wash my clothes, and empty my pots in it. Good or bad, here I have always been, it is too late for me to change; and, after all, nothing can happen worse than what has happened before. Even if the house is burned down again (for you never can tell), I do not propose to build for all eternity, but here where I have taken root it is not easy to pull me up. I have rebuilt twice, if necessary I can do it ten times more; not that I look upon it as an amusement, but it would be still less amusing to change, and I should be like a man stripped of his skin; there would be no use in offering me a fine new white one; I know it would not fit; it would wrinkle on me or I should burst it. On the whole I prefer the old one.

Now let us add it all up: Wife, children, house; have I reckoned up all my goods? I have kept the best to the last, my trade. I am a carpenter and woodworker, belonging to the brotherhood of St. Anne, and when we have a procession I am the one who carries the staff with the device of a compass on a lyre, and there you may see God's grandmother teaching the little Mary to read, a Virgin full of grace no bigger than your thumb. Armed with hatchet, chisel, and auger, with my plane at hand, I rule over knotted oak and smooth walnut from my workbench, and the result rests with me—and with my customer's pocket. Many shapes lie hidden there! To rouse Beauty sleeping in the wood, her lover must penetrate to the heart of it, but the loveliness which is unveiled under my plane has no unrealities. You know those slim Dianas of the early Italians, straight behind and before?—a good Burgundy piece is better yet, bronzed, strong, covered like a grapevine with fruit; a fine bulging cupboard, a carved wardrobe, such as Master Hugues Tambin wrought fantastically. I dress my houses with panels, and moldings, and winding staircases in long twists and my furniture is like trained fruit trees, full and robust, sprouting from the wall, made for the very spot where I place it. The best of all is when I can fix on my wood something I see smiling in my mind's eye, a gesture, a movement, a bending back or swelling breast, flowery curves, garlands and grotesques, or when I catch the face of some passerby on the wing and pin it to my plank. The finest thing I ever turned out, the choir stalls in the Church of Montreal, show two men at table drinking and laughing with a jug between them, and two lions snarling over a bone. I did that to please myself and the vicar. To work after a good drink, and drink after good work, is my idea of a fine life! ... I see all sorts of useless grumblers around me; they say I have picked out a queer time to shout in, that we are in a sad state now; but no state is sad, there are only dreary people, and I am not one of them, the Lord be praised! Men ill-treat you and rob you?—so it ever shall be. I would wager my neck that centuries from now our great-grandnephews will be equally keen to claw and scratch each other's eyes. No doubt they will have thought of forty new ways to do the trick better than we, but I bet they cannot find out a new way to drink, and I defy them to do better in the line than I. Who knows what those fellows will be up to in four hundred years? The Curé of Meudon had an herb, the wonderful Pantagruelion; maybe thanks to that our descendants will visit the glimpses of the moon, the forge of the thunder, and the sluices of the rain; perhaps stay a while in Heaven to sport with the gods. Good enough! I'll go with them. Are they not the fruit of my loins, and seed of my own sowing? The future is yours, my sons—but I like it better where I am, it is safer on the whole, and how can I be sure that wine will be as good in four centuries from now? My wife reproaches me because I am too fond of a spree, but I own that I can't bear to lose a trick. I take what the gods provide, good food, good drink, pretty plump pleasures, and then those soft tender downy things that a man enjoys in a day dream, that divine do-nothing state where all things are possible, where you are young, handsome, triumphant, with the world at your feet, and you work miracles, hear the grass grow and talk with trees, beasts, and gods. There is one old chum that never goes back on me, my other self, my friend,—my work. How good it is to stand before the bench with a tool in my hand and then saw and cut, plane, shave, curve, put in a peg, file, twist and turn the strong fine stuff, which resists yet yields—soft smooth walnut, as soft to my fingers as fairy flesh; the rosy bodies or brown limbs of our wood-nymphs which the hatchet has stripped of their robe. There is no pleasure like the accurate hand, the clever big fingers which can turn out the most fragile works of art, no pleasure like the thought which rules over the forces of the world, and writes the ordered caprices of its rich imagination on wood, iron, and stone. I am king of a magic realm; my field yields me its flesh, my vine its blood, and to serve my art the elves of the sap push out the fair limbs of the trees, lengthen and fatten them until they are polished fit for my caresses. My hands are docile workmen, directed by their foreman, my old brain here, and he plays the game as I like it, for is he not my servant too? Was ever man better served than I? I'm a true little king, and really must drink my majesty's health, and that of my faithful subjects, for I am not ungrateful. Blessed be the day when I saw the light! How many glorious things there are on this round ball, things which smile at you, and taste sweet. Life is good, by the Lord! I always hunger for more, no matter how much I stuff myself; but I am afraid that I shall make myself sick; sometimes, I give you my word, my mouth fairly waters before the feast spread for me by the earth and the sun.

But while I am boasting, old boy, the sun has gone, and left my little world all chilled. That beastly old winter has pushed his way into my very room, so that the pen trembles in my stiff fingers; there is actually ice in my glass, and my nose is blue. Detestable color! it makes me think of graveyards. I hate anything pale. — Hullo, wake up! St. Martin is ringing his chimes; it is Candlemas today. "When the days begin to lengthen, the cold begins to strengthen," does it indeed? then we must do likewise, we will go out and meet it face to face. It is cold, and no mistake; my cheeks sting with the frost needles, and the north wind lies in wait at the corner to catch me by the beard, but I am beginning to warm up, thank the Lord! and my complexion is once more brilliant. I like the ring of the hard ground under my feet, it makes me as merry as a grig, but what ails all these folks that they are so pinched and wretched-looking?

"Well, Mrs. Neighbor, what has put you out? It's the wind, hey, rumpling up your skirts? I don't blame him, young rascal! I wish I were young myself; he knows the right spot — greedy scamp! he picks out the toothsome morsels. Have patience, old girl; live and let live. And where are you running, as if the devil were after you? To church? God will always get the better of Satan. Those who weep will rejoice, and frost will burn. Now you are laughing yourself? good, good; I am on the run for church too, yes I am off to Mass like you, only it will not be said by the Curé, — Mass in the fields is what I mean."

I stop at my daughter's first to get my little Glodie, for we walk together every day. Best little friend that she is to me! my lambling, my little chirping frog, just five years old; as wide-awake as a mouse and keen as mustard. She comes running to meet me, for she knows I always have a lot of new stories for her, it is hard to say which she loves most; — so we go on hand in hand.

"Come along, darling, to meet the lark."

"What lark?"

"It is Candlemas. Did you never hear that today the lark comes back to us out of the skies?"

"What did he do up there?"

"He went to look for fire."

"What fire?"

"Fire to make sunshine, fire to boil the kettle."

"Did the fire fly away then?"

"Why yes, on All Saints' Day. In November every year it leaves us to go and warm up the stars."

"And how do we get him back again?"

"We send three little birds to fetch him."

"Oh, do tell me!"

There she is trotting along the road, all warmly snuggled in a jacket of soft white wool, looking like a little robin in her red hood. She doesn't mind the cold, not she! but her fat cheeks are like rosy apples, and her little nose runs.

"Ah, this little candle needs the snuffers, is that because of Candlemas? and the lights in Heaven?"

"Oh, Grandfather, do tell about the three little birds."

"Three little birds set off on a journey, three bold companions; the Wren, the Red-Breast, and their friend the Lark; Wren, brisk as quicksilver and proud as Artaban, soon spied a bright spark floating in the air. He snapped at it, crying, 'I have it! I, I, I!' The others joined in the same cry, but as Wren flew down he screamed, 'Fire! I am burning!' He rolled the hot morsel from one corner of his beak to the other, and at last his tongue was peeling, and he could bear no more, so he spit it out and hid it under his little wings. Did you ever notice the red spots, and his frizzled feathers?—Red-Breast rushed to help him. He seized the spark of fire and put it carefully on his soft waistcoat, but the fine waistcoat got red and redder and poor Red-Breast screamed, 'Enough—my clothes are burning.' Then came the Lark, the brave little friend, catching the spark which was flying off to Heaven, and quick, prompt, and swift as an arrow she fell to the earth; then with her little beak she buried the bright spark of sunshine in the frozen ground, and, oh, how glad it was to feel it!" My story came to an end, and it was Glodie's turn to tell one; then when we got outside the town, I took her on my back as we climbed the hill. The sky is gray and the snow creaks under our wooden shoes; the delicate little skeletons of the trees and bushes are all wadded with white, and the smoke mounts up straight from the cottage chimneys slow and blue. There is no sound but the chirp of my little frog,—but here we are at the top. Below at our feet lies my town, wrapped about by the lazy Yonne and the trifling Beuvron, like silver ribbons, covered with snow, frozen, chilled and shivering, yet somehow it warms my heart only to look at the place.

City of bright reflections and rolling hills, the soft lines of tilled slopes surround you like the twisted straw of a nest. The undulations of five or six ranges of wooded mountains in the distance are faintly blue like the sea, but it is not the perfidious element which overthrew Ulysses and his fleet. Here are no storms, no ambuscades; all is calm, save that here and there a breath seems to swell the breast of a hill. From the crest of one wave to the other, the roads run deliberately straight, leaving, as it were, a wake behind them, and beyond the edge of the waters, far away the spires of St. Marie Madeleine of Vézelay rise like masts. Close by, in a bend of the Yonne, you can see the rocks of Basseville sticking up through the underbrush like boars' tusks, and in the center of the circle of hills the town, carelessly adorned, leans over the water with her gardens, her buildings, her rags, and her jewels. Here is filth; but here also is the harmony of her long limbs, and her head crowned with the pierced tower. You see the snail admires his shell. The chimes of the church float up from the valley and their pure voices spread like a crystal flood through the thin clear air. As I stand happily drinking in the music, suddenly a ray of sunshine breaks through the gray mantle which hides the sky, and Glodie claps her hands, crying:

"Grandad, I hear him — the lark, the lark!" Her dear little fresh voice made me laugh as I kissed her and said:

"I hear him too, my sweet little spring Lark!"

II
The Siege
or
The Lamb, the Shepherd, and the Wolf

"Three lambs of Chamoux can put to flight
Any wolf who comes in the night."

MY cellar will soon be empty, for the soldiers whom our lord the Duke
of Nevers sent to defend us have tapped my last cask, so there is no
time to be lost. I must drink with them. Taken in the right spirit, I do
not object to being ruined, and it is not by any means the first time,
but God send it may be the last! The soldiers, good fellows that they
are, felt worse than I did when I told them that the liquor was running
low. Some of my neighbors take such things tragically, but that is not
my way. I have been too often to the play in the course of my life to be
impressed by clowns. Since I was born into this world, how many of
these masqueraders I have seen! Swiss, German, Gascons, Lorrainers;
all dogs of war, with harness on their back and arms at their side; vict-
ual swallowers, hungry hounds, always ready to devour us fellows. No
one can tell for what they are fighting. Today it is for the King; tomorrow for the League; now for the Black-beetles; now for the Protestants;
but one side is as good as another. The best of them is not worth the
powder it would take to shoot them. What difference does it make to
us which robber ruffles it at court? And as for the way they appeal to
Heaven, ye gods and little fishes! The Lord is old enough to know what
to do. If your hide itches, scratch yourself. God is not left-handed that
He should need you, and He acts as He pleases. But the worst of all
is when they make it out that I too must try to pull the wool over His
eyes! With all due reverence, Lord, I can say without boasting, You
and I meet several times in the twenty-four hours; that is, if the good
old French saying is true, "He who can good wine afford has a chance
to see the Lord!" But these frauds say something else that would never
enter my head. They say that I know Thee like a brother; that I am to
carry out Thy will; but Thou wilt do me the justice to admit that if I
leave Heaven in peace I only ask that it will do as much for me. Each
of us has enough to do to keep his own house in order, Thou in Thy
big world, and I in my little one. Since Thou hast made me free, Lord,

Thou shouldst be free also! But these fools want me to mix myself up in Thy concerns, to speak in Thy name, to decide how men are to take Thy Sacraments, and if they do otherwise, to declare them my enemies and Thine. Mine indeed! By no means; I have none; for all men are my friends. Let them fight, then, if it likes them, I am out of the game;—that is if they will let me alone, but that is just what the rascals will not do. If I will not be the enemy of one of them they will both set on me, so between two fires I must be hit. Here goes then! I will get to fighting myself, for I would rather on the whole be first anvil and then hammer, than anvil all the time. I wish some one would tell me why such brutes came into the world? marauders, politicians, great nobles, who bleed our France while they blow her trumpet and stick their fingers in her pocket. They are not content to devour our own substance, but they must needs attack the stores of others. They threaten Germany, cast the eye of longing on Italy, and even poke their noses into the harem of the Grand Turk! They would like to absorb half the earth, they who would not know enough to grow cabbages on it! Never mind, old boy, do not let us fret over it, since all is for the best as it is until the happy day when we can make it better in the shortest possible time. It is a poor beast that is of no use, and I heard a story once about the good Lord;— (Pardon, Almighty, my head is full of Thee today)—He was walking with Peter in one of our suburbs, Béyant,[1] and a woman sat cooling her heels on her doorstep. She looked so bored that our Father, out of the goodness of His heart, drew a hundred fleas from his pocket and threw them to her, saying, "There is something to amuse yourself with, my daughter!" The woman roused herself to see what she could catch, and every time she caught one of the beasts she laughed for joy.

Through this same charity, no doubt, Heaven has bestowed on us those big two-legged beasts who shear our wool. They keep us busy, so let us be joyful. Vermin is a sign of health, they say, (and our masters are certainly vermin), so I say again, be joyful, my friends, for if that is true no one is healthier than we are. Let me whisper a word in your ear; we shall have the best of it if we are patient; cold and frost, good-for-nothings at court or in camp, will have their day. They too will pass, but the good ground remains and we are there to enrich it. One crop will put all to rights, meanwhile let us suck up the bottom of my cask, if only to make room for the vintage of next year.

My daughter, Martine, said to me one day, "You are a braggart. To hear you one would think that you only work with your mouth, idling, gossiping like a bell-clapper, yawning, and staring; you pretend to live only for feasting, and are ready to drink up the sea; yet really you cannot be happy one day without work. You want people to think you are careless, wasteful, and idle as a cock-chafer; you pretend not to count

---

[1] Bethléem, a suburb of Clamecy.

what goes into your purse nor what comes out of it, but it would make you ill if your day was not marked off hour by hour like a striking clock, and you know to a penny what you have spent since last Easter, and the man does not live who ever got ahead of you. Dear old stupid head, innocent lamb that he is! 'Three lambs of Chamoux can put to flight any wolf who comes in the night.'"

I laughed, but did not answer Madame Saucy-Tongue. Besides, the child is right, though she ought not to say so, but a woman only hides what she knows nothing about. It is true that she understands me, for did I not make her?

Come, Colas Breugnon, you may as well confess you commit many follies, but you are not a fool.

Like every one else, by Jove, you have a simpleton up your sleeve who shows when you like, but he is tucked away out of sight when you need a clear head and free hands. Like all Frenchmen, you have the sense of reason and order so firmly fixed in your noddle that you can let yourself go safely. The only danger is for those poor fools who look at you with an open mouth and try to imitate you. Fine speeches, sounding verse, daring projects, are all enjoyable. They exalt and kindle the soul. But *we* only burn up our chips, and leave the big logs in order on the wood-pile. My reason sits at ease and looks on at the freaks of my imagination, and all for my own amusement. The world is my theater, and without stirring from my seat, I am the play; I can applaud Matamore or Francatrippa; I witness tourneys and royal processions, I shout "At him again!" when a man gets his head cracked all for our good pleasure, and to add to it, I pretend to take part in the farce and to believe in it only just enough to keep up the joke. No more, you may be sure. That is the way to listen to fairy tales and not to them only! There is Some One up there above the clouds for whom we have a great respect when the procession passes through our streets with cross and banner, chanting the *Oremus;* we drape the walls of our houses with white—but between ourselves?—Shut up, chatterer, you go too far! Be deaf, Lord, to my folly, and accept my humble service.

The end of February.
An ass having eaten the grass in the meadow, said, "There is no further need to watch it," and so went to eat (I mean watch) in another field near by. The garrison of the Duke of Nevers left us today. I was really proud of our cookery when I looked at them, for they were as fat as seals. We parted with smiles in our hearts and on our lips; they with the kindest wishes for the next season, hoping our crops would be good and our vines safe from the frost.

"Work hard, dear uncle," said my guest, the Sergeant Fiacre Bolacre, (it is his pet name for me and one which I deserve, for that relation gives a good ration.) "Go prune your vines, no matter how much trouble it costs you, and next St. Martin's Day we will come back to drink the wine." Gallant fellows! Always ready to help an honest man with his bottle.

Now that they are gone, what a weight is off our shoulders! The neighbors are carefully uncovering their little hiding places. They have gone about for the last few days with long faces complaining of hunger as if a wolf were gnawing at their vitals, and now from the straw of the garret, or the earth of the cellar, they have dug out something to feed the beast. Those who bewailed their destitute state the loudest, the worst beggars of them all, found means to tuck their best wine away in some corner. I don't know how it happened, but scarcely had my guest, Fiacre Bolacre, left me, (I went with him to the end of the Jews' quarter,) when I suddenly remembered a small cask of Chablis left by mistake under the dunghill in a good warm place. Of course this upset me dreadfully! You can easily understand that, but when harm is done, if it is well done, one must bear it as best one can, and I bear it well. "Bolacre, my dear nephew, you don't know what nectar you have lost, ah-h! It is not all loss to you though, my good friend, for here's your health in it!"

We all began visiting from house to house, showing what we had found in our cellars, congratulating each other, and winking like the Roman Augurs. We spoke also of our injuries and losses, (losses of our lasses,) and as sometimes the misfortunes of one's neighbors are an amusing consolation, we all inquired solicitously for the health of Vincent Pluviaut's wife. (By an extraordinary chance, after a body of troops has passed through the town this brave Frenchwoman usually has to let out her belt.)

We congratulated Pluviaut, and praised him for his public services in these trying times, and by way of a joke, meaning no harm, I gave him a friendly tap, telling him he was lucky to have a house full now that all the others were empty. Every one laughed, of course, but not too loud, just enough to be heard, but Pluviaut did not much like it, and told me I had better look after my own wife. "Ah," said I, "as far as she is concerned I may sleep in peace. No one is likely to rob me of my treasure." And, do you know, they all agreed with me!

Feast days will soon be upon us, so, though somewhat short of means, we must live up to our reputation and that of the town. What would the world say if Shrove-Tuesday caught Clamecy without its justly celebrated meat-balls? You can hear the grease frying, and sniff the delicious fragrance in the streets. The flapjacks fairly hop from the pan for my little Glodie! Now the drums go "rub-a-dub," and the flutes "twee-wee," as amid cheers and shouts the "Gentlemen from Judaea" come on their car to visit "Rome."[2] First appears the band; then the hal-

---

[2] "Judæa" is the nickname given to the suburb of Bethléem, or Béyant, where the raftsmen and boatmen of Clamecy live. "Rome" is the upper town, which gets its name on account of the stairs, called "Old Rome," which go down from the church of Saint Martin to the suburb of Beuvron.

berdiers, and the crowd actually falls back before the great noses they wear. Some are shaped like trumpets, or lances, there are snouts like hunting-horns or pea-shooters, noses stuck full of spikes, like a chestnut burr, or with a bird perched on the tip. They hustle the passers-by, and tickle the ribs of the squealing girls; and at last comes the Nose King, scattering all before him like a battering-ram with his great proboscis which rests on a gun-carriage like a bombard.

Then comes the car of Lent, Emperor of the Fish-eaters. Their masks are pale green, skinny, and chilled-looking. They shiver under hoods, or heads of fishes. One has a perch, or a carp, in each hand; another brandishes a gudgeon stuck on a fork; a third wears a hat like a pike's head, with a roach dangling from its mouth, and little fishes falling all around. It is enough to give a man a surfeit. Some stick their fingers into their jaws and try to force down eggs too big to swallow. To right and left, high up on the car, are masks of owls and monks and fishermen dangling their lines over the heads of urchins, who jump up like goats to catch at what may be sweetmeats or perhaps only dirt rolled in sugar. Behind is a dancing devil, dressed like a cook, waving a saucepan and big spoon. Six souls of the damned stick their grinning heads through the rungs of a ladder behind the car, and the devil keeps thrusting his spoonful of disgusting stew at them.

Hurrah! Here come the conquerors, heroes of the day! On a throne built of hams, under a canopy of smoked tongues, comes the queen of the Meat-Balls, crowned with saveloys, while her pudding fingers play coquettishly with the sausages around her neck. She is escorted by her aids, black and white puddings, and little Clamecy balls. They make a fine appearance, as their Colonel Riflandouille leads them to victory, armed with fat and greasy spits and larding needles. I like best of all those dignified old fellows with bellies like a great soup-pot, or with a body made of bread crust, bearing gifts like the Magi: a pig's head, a bottle of black wine, or mustard from Dijon. Now to the sound of brass cymbals, skimmers, and dishpans, comes the King of Dupes, mounted on a donkey, and greeted with shouts of laughter. It is our friend, Vincent Pluviaut, who has been elected. Riding backwards, a turban on his head, a goblet in his hand, he is listening to his body-guard of horned imps, who prance along with pitchforks or rods on their shoulders, shouting out in good plain French the tale of his glory. He is too wise to betray his pride and tosses off a bumper with a careless air, but when they pass a house as distinguished as his own, he cries, "Here's your good health, Brother!" as he raises his glass.

The procession ends with lovely Spring; a young girl, fresh and smiling, with smooth brow and fair curling locks crowned with yellow primroses, and wearing across her slender breast a chain of green catkins plucked from the young nut trees. The pouch by her side and the basket in her hands are brimming with good things. Her delicate eyebrows arch over her wide blue eyes; her sharp little teeth show as she opens her mouth like a round "O" to sing in her treble pipe about the swallow who will soon be here again. Four white oxen draw her chariot, and by her side are plump maids, well-developed, rounded and graceful, and little girls at the awkward age, sticking out like young trees in all directions. Something is lacking to each one; they are no beauties as yet, but toothsome morsels for the wolf in future none the less. Some carry migratory birds in cages, and some dip their hands in the basket of Spring and shower treasures on the crowd; cakes, sweetmeats and surprises, out of which fall hats and vests, mottoes telling your fortune, lovers' couplets, horns of plenty, or of ill luck.

When they come to the market-place, near the tower, the maids jump from the car and dance with the clerks and students, while Shrove-Tuesday, Lent, and King Pluviaut continue their triumphal progress, pausing every few feet to chaff the people, or toss off a glass,

> "Let your goblets chink —
> Drink, Drink, Drink!
> Shall we go without it?
>   No!
> See the bottom of your glass
> Or we shall write you down an ass!"

After all, too much soaking is bad for one's tongue and one's wit, so I leave friend Vincent and his escort drawing more corks, and make for the open fields. The day is really too fine to waste between walls. My old friend Chamaille, the vicar, has come up from his village in a little donkey-cart to dine with the Archdeacon of St. Martin. As he asked me to go with him for part of the way back, we climb into the tail of the cart, little Glodie and I, and off goes the donkey! She is so small that I suggest we shall take her up on the seat between us. As the road stretches out long and white, the sun looks drowsy, as if he meant to warm his own chimney corner more than ours. The donkey drowses also and stops as if to think, so the vicar shouts indignantly, in his great voice like a bell, "Madelon!" Donkey jumps, stirs her spindle-shanks, zigzags from one rut to another, then stops again to meditate, regardless of our objurgations. "Beast of ill-omen, if you had not the sign of the Cross on your back, I would break this stick on you," roars the vicar, all the time basting her flanks with his cane.

We stopped to rest ourselves at the inn, just where the road turns to go down to the white hamlet of Armes which lies looking at its fair reflection in the water. Near by in the field we see some girls dancing round an old nut tree whose great withered branches stretch toward the pale sky. They have been carrying Shrove-Tuesday pancakes to the magpies. "Come and dance too!" they cry.

"Look, Glodie, look at the magpie way up there; look at her white breast over the edge of the nest! She is peeping out to see what she can see, and she has made her little house open all around so that nothing can escape her sharp eye and her chattering tongue. The wind blows through it, so that she is wet and cold, but as long as she sees all that goes on, she is satisfied. Now she is out of humor and seems to say, 'Rude people, be off with your presents. Do you think if I wanted your cakes I could not pick them up in your very houses? There is no fun in eating things that are given to you; stolen dainties are the only ones I relish.'

"Grandad, why do they give her pancakes all tied up with ribbons? Why do they bring good-wishes to that old pilferer?"

"Because, darling, in this world it is better to be on good terms with evildoers."

"What's that, Colas Breugnon? What idea are you putting in the child's head?" growled the vicar.

"I am not holding it up for her admiration. I only tell her that is what every one does, you yourself, vicar, among the first. Don't stare at me like that, you know when you have a parishioner who knows everything, sees everything, pokes her nose into everything, and is as full of spite as a nut is full of meat you would stuff her mouth with cakes, if that would keep her quiet."

"Lord, if that were enough," sighed the vicar. "I am really not fair to old magpie, she is better than some women, and her tongue is sometimes of use!"

"What is it good for, Grandfather?"

"She screams when the wolf is near." And at these words, all of a sudden the bird begins to cry, swear, and blaspheme. She flaps her wings, flies, and pours out abuse toward I don't know who or what down in the valley near Armes. At the edge of the wood her feathered companions, Chariot the jay, and the crow Colas, answer sharply in the same irritated key. The villagers laugh and cry, "Wolf!" No one believes it, but still they think they will go and look (it is good to trust, but better to know), and what do you think they see? A band of armed men coming up the hill at a trot. We know them only too well; they are those rascals, the soldiers of Vézelay, who knowing our town is off its guard, think they will catch the bird on its nest. (Not this old magpie, however.)

We did not stop to look at them, as you may well believe! Every man for himself, was the cry, and we all tumbled over each other. We took to our heels by the road, across the fields; some on all fours, and some sliding on the hinder side of their anatomy. We three jumped into the donkey-cart; and, as if she understood it all, off went Madelon like an arrow from the bow. The vicar forgot in his excitement the consideration due to a donkey which has a cross marked on its back, and belabored her with all his might. We rushed along through a crowd of people screaming like blackbirds, and entered Clamecy first by a head, covered with dust and glory, but with the rest of the fugitives hard on our heels. Madelon scarcely touched the ground as we flew through Béyant at full gallop, the cart bouncing, the vicar beating, and shouting at the top of his lungs, "The enemy is upon us!"

People laughed at first as they saw us flying past them, but it did not take them long to catch the idea, and the town was soon like an ant-heap when you thrust a stick into it. Every one got to work, running in and out. Men armed themselves; women packed up their goods, piling things into baskets and wheelbarrows; and all the folks in the suburbs, abandoning their homes, fled to the shelter of the town walls. The masquers rushed to the ramparts, still wearing their costumes, masks, horns, claws, and paunches; some as Gargantua, some as Beelzebub, armed with gaffs and harpoons; and so when the advance guard of Vézelay reached the walls, the drawbridges were raised, and only some poor devils remained on the other side of the moat, who having nothing to lose made no effort to save it, and poor old King Pluviaut, deserted by his escort, full as a tick, like the Patriarch Noah, sat snoring on his beast, holding on by the tail.

Here is where you can see the advantage of having Frenchmen for your enemies. Germans, Swiss, or English, do their thinking through their fists, and are so thickheaded that it takes them till Christmas to understand what was told them on All Saints' Day. I would not have given a button for poor Pluviaut's chance with such people as these. They would have thought we were playing a joke on them, but no words are necessary between *us*. If we come from Lorraine, Touraine, Champagne, or Bretagne, geese from Beauce, asses from Beaune, or rabbits from Vézelay, a good joke hits us all in the right spot, no matter how much we may pound and beat each other. When they caught sight of our old Silenus, their whole camp burst out laughing. They laughed all over their faces, with their throats, with all their hearts, and even their stomachs, and by St. Rigobert! to see the way they laughed set us off too, all along our line. Like Ajax, and Hector the Trojan, we hurled gay defiance at each other across the moat. Our remarks, however, had much more snap than theirs. If I were not so busy, I would write them down, but if you can put up with it, I mean to include them in a collection I have been making for the last dozen years of the best jokes, quips, and witticisms that I have heard, said, or read, in the course of my pilgrimage through this vale of tears. I would not lose it for a kingdom. It makes me crack my old sides only to think of it. There now! I have made a great blot on my paper.

When the noise had subsided, it was time to fight, (nothing is so restful when one has been talked to death), but neither side was keen for it. Their surprise had failed, and we were well protected. They did not care much about scrambling up our walls (you may break your bones at that game) but something had to be done at any cost; it did not matter much what, so a little powder was burned, some petards let off at random, from which the sparrows were the only sufferers. We sat with our backs to the wall inside the parapet, waiting while their plums flew over our heads for the right moment to discharge our own without taking aim, (there is no sense in exposing one's self too much).

When we heard their prisoners squalling we ventured to look out. They had caught a dozen men and women from Béyant and were beating them as they stood in a row, with their faces turned to the wall. The poor devils were not much hurt, but they screamed like curlews. Being safe enough ourselves, we slipped down along the ramparts and brandished pikes over the walls, on which we had stuck hams, saveloys, and black-puddings. We could hear the besiegers uttering yells of hunger and rage, and how that did put new life into us! To squeeze out the last drop (for there is never too much of a good thing), when it grew late we set out tables in the open air on the slopes, sheltered by the wall, and loaded them with victuals and drink. There we had a noisy feast, singing and drinking to Shrove-Tuesday. The outsiders nearly went out of their skins with fury, and so that day went off gaily, and no harm done. There was only one drawback. When Gueneau de Pousseaux, that big fool! got too mellow, nothing would do but he must walk on top of the wall with his glass in his hand, just to defy them, and they knocked his head and his glass into splinters with a musket ball. This did not much bother us, but to make it even, we wounded one or two of them, for there can be no festivity, you know, without a little broken crockery. Chamaille waited till nightfall before leaving the town to go home. In vain we all said, "Old friend, you risk your neck. Wait here till it's all over; God will take care of your parishioners." He answered:

"My place is with my flock. God would be maimed without me, for I am truly His right arm. But I will not fail Him, you may swear."

"I believe you," said I. "You gave full proof of it when the Huguenots attacked your church, and you threw a great lump of plaster at their Captain Papiphage and knocked him over."

"That was a surprise for him, miscreant that he was," said he. "For me too, really. I mean no harm and hate to see blood flow; it disgusts me, but the devil alone knows what gets into a man when he is among hot-heads. He becomes a wolf."

"That is true," said I, "you lose what little sense you have when you are in a crowd. A hundred wise men make a fool, and a hundred sheep a wolf. But tell me, Vicar, how can you reconcile two codes — that of the man who lives alone with his conscience and wants peace for himself and all the world, and that of men in the mass, who make a virtue out of war and wickedness. Which of these is of God?"

"That is a very silly question! Both. Everything comes from God."

"Well, then He doesn't know His own mind. Or rather I believe He cannot do as He likes. It is easy enough to manage one man, — there is no difficulty about that, but when He has a crowd to deal with, that is another pair of shoes. What can one do against many? So man falls back on his Mother Earth, who whispers to him of fleshly things. In the old legend, if you remember, there are times when men become wolves, and then get into their old skins again. Ah! my friend, there is more truth in many an old song than in your Mass-book. Every man in the country wears his wolf skin; States, Kings, and Ministers may dress themselves up with shepherd's crooks as much as they please, and claim descent, like the hypocrites they are, from your Good Shepherd; they are really all lynxes, bulls, jaws, and bellies, always crying for food, and for the best of reasons; they must satisfy the hunger of the earth."

"You are a raving heathen," said Chamaille. "God sends the wolves like the rest, and He does all things well. Did you never hear that the Blessed Virgin had a little garden where cabbages grew, and Jesus, they say, made the wolf to keep off the goats and the kids? No doubt He was right, and we can only bow to His will. Why should we complain of the strong? It would be a thousand times worse if the weak were raised to power, so in conclusion all are for the best, sheep and wolves alike. The sheep need the wolves to protect them, and the wolves need the sheep, still more, for we all must eat. So now, Colas, off I go to my cabbages." He confided Madelon tenderly to my care, tucked up his gown, grasped his cudgel, and made off; though the night was dark and moonless.

We were not quite so merry for the next few days. We had foolishly stuffed ourselves the first evening, just to show off and from stupid greediness, so there was but little left of our provisions. We had to draw in our belts, which was soon done, but we still had some swagger in us. When the puddings were all gone, we made some stuffed with bran and tarred strings which we stuck on a pike and dangled before the enemy. The rogues soon saw through it, though, for a ball caught one of our puddings fair in the middle, and who had the laugh on his side then? Not we, I vow, and to cap the climax when these robbers saw that we were fishing over the top of our wall, they stretched nets from the locks up and down the river to catch the fry. Our Archbishop reprimanded them for bad Christians who would not let us keep Lent, but in vain, so we had to fall back on our own fat.

We might of course have implored the Duke of Nevers to come and help us, but to tell the truth we were not anxious to have his troops quartered on us again. It cost less to have the enemy outside the walls than the friend within, so the best way was to keep quiet as long as we could get along without them, and the enemy on his side was prudent enough not to send for them. "Two is company, three is none," so we began negotiations, but without undue haste. Both camps led an exemplary life. Early to bed and late to rise, playing bowls all day and drinking. We yawned more from boredom than hunger, and we actually slept so much that we grew fat in spite of our fast. The grown people moved about as little as possible, but it was hard to keep the children in order. These imps were always running, crying, or laughing; always on the go and putting themselves in danger. They would climb the walls, stick out their tongues at the besiegers, and bombard them with stones. They had batteries of squirts, which they made from the elder twigs; slings and sticks;—"Here goes. Hit him in the head!" the little monkeys would cry. Those they struck vowed to be the death of them, and they called out to us that the first child that poked its nose over the top of the wall should be shot. We promised to be careful, but the rogues slipped through our fingers in spite of our scoldings and ear-pullings. Still water runs deep, so one fine evening, (it makes me tremble only to think of it!) I heard a squeal, and if you can believe it, there was that little hypocrite of a Glodie,—witch that she is! my own treasure!—she had slipped down the bank into the ditch. Oh, Lord, I could have whipped her! I was on the wall at one bound, and there we all stood craning over. We made a fine target if the enemy had chosen to shoot at us, but he too was looking at my darling at the bottom of the ditch. Thanks to the Blessed Virgin, she had rolled down gently like a little kitten, and sat there among the flowering grasses, not in the least frightened, and looking up at the two rows of heads above her. She was laughing and making a nosegay. We all laughed too, and Monseigneur de Ragny, the enemy's commander, ordered that no harm be done to the child, and, good fellow that he was, threw her a bag of sugarplums. But you never know what a woman will do next, and while we were all looking at Glodie, Martine rushed to save her lamb and she too fell down the bank, running, slipping, and rolling, her skirts turned up over her head. What a spectacle for the enemy! Immense applause! But nothing daunted, she hugged and slapped her baby. One of the soldiers, carried away by her charms, disobeyed his commanding officer, jumped into the ditch and ran towards her. She stood fast while we threw a broom down to her from the ramparts, seized it bravely, and marched on the enemy.

Whick, whack! The gallant kept his distance, and fled from the field without sound of trumpets. Both camps roared with laughter, and we pulled Martine up, triumphant, with her child in her arms, I on the end of the rope as proud as a peacock.

Since talking is always in season, we took another week for discussion. A rumor was heard that the Duke of Nevers was coming,—a false alarm, but it brought us together and a treaty was drawn up on fairly easy terms. We agreed to pay to the Vézelayans a tenth of our next vintage, for it is always best to promise for the future; one may never get there, and in any case much water runs under the bridge first and much wine into our stomachs.

Both sides were satisfied with each other, and most of all with themselves. Still, it never rains but it pours, and the very next day after the treaty, a sign appeared in the heavens. About ten o'clock it arose and slid across the field of stars toward St. Peters-on-the-Height, like a long serpent. It resembled a sword with a flame on the point, and great tongues of smoke; a hand seemed to grasp the hilt. You could see the five fingers ending in dreadful heads; one was a woman with her hair streaming in the wind, and the width at the hilt of the sword was a span, at the point six or eight rods, and in the middle exactly three rods and two inches. The color was scarlet and violet, and inflamed like a wound in the side. We all stood, our eyes raised to Heaven, our mouths open, our teeth chattering in our heads. In the two camps the question was "To which one did the warning come?" Each of course attributed it to the other, and every man shivered, except me. I was not in the least frightened, for having gone to bed at nine o'clock, I naturally saw nothing. Regularly as the day comes round, I take medicine and go to bed early; when the stomach commands I obey without question. Every one, however, told me all about the portent, so I write it down, for it is the same as if I had seen it.

As soon as peace was signed, friends and foes betook themselves once more to feasting, and as by this time we had come to the middle of Lent, we let ourselves go. It was a great day, I can tell you. Throngs of people came pouring in from the neighboring villages, bringing their provisions as well as mouths to eat them with, and tables were spread the whole length of the ramparts. Three young pigs were served, roasted whole, stuffed with spiced boar's meat and heron's liver. There were hams, smoked and perfumed with juniper; rabbit and pork pies, simply reeking with garlic and laurel; our own meat-balls and tripe, pikes and snails, jugged hare so fat that our noses fed on them first; calves-head that melted in the mouth; and heaps of peppery lobsters enough to set your throat on fire. On top of all, to cool it off, salads with plenty of vinegar; and then bumpers of the best vintages from Chapotte, Mandre, and Vaufilloux. For dessert we had curds and cream to slip gently down our throats, and biscuits with which we sopped up a full glass at one mouthful. As long as a scrap remained not one of us let go, and the Lord gave us strength to squeeze all these dishes and drinks into our small bread-baskets. There was a great contest between two eating champions. The Vézelayans put up their hermit—Court-Oreille from St. Martin's at Vézelay; (he was the man, we are told, who first discovered that an ass must have his tail in the air before he can bray); ours, (hermit, I mean not ass,) was Dom Hennequin, who declared that he had such a hatred for cold water that he believed he must have been a carp or a pike in some former existence and been forced to swallow too much of it. Well, when the Vézelayans and Clamecyans left off eating at last, they loved each other more than they did at first; since a man's fine qualities come out strong at table, and he who loves good cheer is my brother. While we were settling our dinner on the best of good terms, what should turn up but the re-enforcements sent by our Duke to protect us? We burst out laughing, and both sides politely requested them to go home. What could they do? So they went off rather crestfallen, like dogs chased by sheep, while we hugged each other and cried out:

"What fools we were to fight for these people! Our protectors, forsooth! They would stir up enemies if we had none, in faith, just for the sake of defending us. God keep us from our keepers, we can look out for ourselves. Silly sheep that we are, we should be safe enough if wolves were all that threatened us, — but who will save us from the shepherd?"

III
The Vicar of Brèves

Early in April.

As soon as the roads were clear of our unwelcome visitors, I decided to
go at once and see Chamaille in his village; not that I was really anxious
about him, for he knows how to take good care of himself, but all the
same nothing is so reassuring as to see with one's own eyes, — besides
my legs wanted stretching. So off I started without a word to any one.
The river flowed at the foot of the wooded hills and I followed the river,
whistling as I went. A soft spring rain came pattering down, now ceas-
ing, now falling again, dropping like beads from the young leaves, and
in the thickets I could hear the cry of an enamored squirrel. Geese were
feeding in the meadow, the blackbirds sang fit to crack their throats,
and the little thrush trilled tipu'ti tipu', — Paillard, the notary at Dornecy, is a great friend of mine, so I thought I would stop and see him,
for he, Chamaille, and I are as inseparable as the Graces. I found him
in his study making notes on the weather, his recent dreams, and the
political situation; close beside him lay the manual "De Legibus," and
also the "Prophecies of Nostradamus." When a man spends his life shut
up between four walls, his mind is all the more eager to fly forth into
dream spaces and the forests of memory; and since he cannot rule this
terrestrial ball, he tries to peer into the future of the world. They say all
is known beforehand, and I can well believe it, but I must confess that I
have never had much luck in predicting the future until after the event.
Dear old Paillard fairly shone with joy when he saw me, and the house
shook with our peals of laughter. I love the very sight of him. He is a
little man, inclined to stoutness; his broad face is pockmarked, his nose
red, and his little eyes dance with cunning. He is always growling and
complaining of everything and everybody, but at bottom good-natured
and full of fun, and more of a joker really than I am myself. He loves
to get off the most awful whoppers with a perfectly straight face, and
at table he is a sight to behold invoking Comus and Momus, singing a
good song, and emptying his bottle. He was enchanted to see me, and
there we stood like two children hand in hand. His are large and thick,
but adroit, like the rest of him, and clever as the devil with all kinds of
tools. He is a bookbinder and carpenter, and declares that everything
in his house is the work of his own hands; not much beauty perhaps
to boast of, but good or bad it is all characteristic of him. He began as

usual by finding fault right and left, and so to take the opposite side I praised the world in general, for it is a favorite joke of his to call me "so much the better," and I retort by calling him "so much the worse." He always has many complaints to make of his clients, and with some reason, for they are by no means prompt in the matter of payment; some of them have owed him money for thirty-five years and he has taken no steps to collect his bills, however much it would be to his interest. Some of his debtors pay when they happen to think of it, but generally in kind; a dozen eggs, a pair of chickens; — that is the usual custom, and it would be thought insulting if he insisted on his money. I suppose he would do the same in their place so he submits, growling.

Luckily he has enough to live on, a nice round sum getting rounder every year, for he is an old bachelor with few expenses, no extravagances, and as for the pleasures of the table, nature has spread her board lavishly in our fields. We have vineyards, orchards, game, and fish in abundance, so there are but two ways for Paillard to spend his money: he buys books, which he likes to show at a distance, for he is chary of lending, and then there are the new spectacles from Holland with which he loves to look at the lady in the moon, sly dog.

He has put up a sort of scaffolding in the roof of his house among the chimneys and from there he carefully studies the movements of the heavenly bodies, and tries to discover the course of our destinies, little as he understands them. To tell the truth he does not really believe in all this, but he likes to persuade himself that he does, and there I agree with him, for what can be more charming than to look out at the stars as if from our window, just as we see fair ladies in the streets, — we imagine a story about them, some romantic adventure, it may not be true, but it is at least amusing — We had much to say to each other about the portent; that terrible bloody sword which had been seen in the heavens during the night of the previous Sunday and each interpreted it according to his own idea, insisting most positively that his view was the right one. After all we found that neither of us had so much as set eyes on it, for the astrologer unluckily had chosen that very evening to fall asleep at his instrument; and thus we were perfectly delighted to find ourselves companions in misfortune and foolishness. Having determined not to mention this incident to Chamaille, we set out across country, admiring the young shoots on the bushes, the pink buds, the birds making their nests, and a hawk slowly circling above the plain. We had a great deal of fun as we went along, over an old joke that we had once played on Chamaille; we shut a blackbird up in a cage, and worked day and night to teach him a Huguenot song, and when he had it well in his head, we turned him loose in the vicar's garden. His new accomplishment was soon picked up by all the other blackbirds in the village, and they sang so loud as to disturb Chamaille at his devotions. He swore, crossing himself, that the devil was loose in his garden, then tried to exorcise him, and finally took aim with an arquebus from behind the shutters, and shot the evil spirit; but in the bottom of his heart he must have had some doubts, for having killed the devil he then proceeded to eat him. Our walking and talking brought us at last to Brèves, which seemed to be half asleep. We peeped into the houses as we went by; the sun was streaming in through the open doors, but we did not see a human being except one urchin enjoying the fresh air on the edge of a ditch. We strolled on arm in arm through the narrow street, encumbered with straw and filth, till, as we got near the center of the town, we began to hear a buzzing like the sound of a swarm of angry bees; and when we came out on the market-place it was packed with people gesticulating and shouting at the top of their lungs. Chamaille was standing at his garden gate purple with rage, and he too was screaming and shaking his fist in the faces of his parishioners. All this was perfectly unintelligible to us, for we could only catch a word here and there in the midst of the tumult of voices. "Caterpillars, — locusts, — field-mice, — cum Spiritu tuo!" Here Chamaille's voice struck in. "No! nothing shall induce me to go!" Retort from the crowd, "Devil take it, are you our vicar or not? You know that you are, and it is your duty to work for us." — "Upstarts! — I am God's servant, not yours!" To put an end to the uproar Chamaille banged the gate in the faces of the foremost, but through the bars we could see him still threatening his people with one hand, while by force of habit the other was raised in the attitude of benediction. We could catch a glimpse of him through the window, square of face and round of belly, and as he could no longer make himself heard above the clamor, we could see the derisive gesture with which he replied; but from that moment the house was closed and turned a blind eye on the street, so the noise gradually died down, the crowd grew thinner, and at last we could get near enough to knock at the door. It was a long time before we could get an answer. "Hi, Vicar!" we called, but there was no reply. "Go to the devil! I am out," came from behind the shutters, and we continued to hammer on the door. "Get out, I tell you! If you don't let my door alone you will get a deluge that will astonish you!" — and the contents of a bucket began to trickle down our backs. "Chamaille!" we called out; "make it wine if you want to soak us." The tempest instantly subsided; and our friend stuck his jolly red face out of the window crying, "Name of a name, boys, is it you? In another minute you would have caught it finely — why didn't you say who you were?" Then he came rushing downstairs. "Come in! come in! Give us your hand, and come upstairs and have a drink; you need it if you are half as hot as I am! It is a real treat to see a civilized human being after those dancing apes; did you see the row they were kicking up? But they can kick as they please, I will not stir one step. Do you know they actually wanted me to go out with the Holy Sacrament? There is a storm coming up too, and the Host and I would both have been soaked; but the idea of treating me as if I were a plowboy! I am no servant of theirs, sacrilegious rascals! I'll teach them to treat God's minister with respect. My business is to cultivate their souls and not their fields."

"What in the world is the matter with you?" said we. "Tell us what has happened." — "Well, come in first," said he, "upstairs where we shall be more comfortable. My throat is as dry as a limekiln, I must have something to drink. Now what do you say to that? You must have tasted worse in your time. But would you believe it, my friends, those brutes actually wanted me to have fasts and feasts every day, and for what do you think? For nothing in the world but insects." — "Insects!" we shouted. "Well, you really must have a bee in your bonnet; are you crazy, or are we?" This was the last straw, and he protested indignantly that it was bad enough to be troubled by all this folly, without being called a fool. "Well then, tell us all about it like a sensible man." — "You will drive me to perdition," said he, wiping the sweat from his brow, "the good Lord and I have been so harried and bothered with all this nonsense, I must try to calm down! — You know these people of mine want their vicar to provide rain and sunshine for them. They jeer at the life eternal and don't keep their souls any cleaner than their feet, but they expect me to make the sun and the moon stand still at their desire. — 'Not too much rain,' they say, 'now a little warm weather and a gentle breeze — no frost for pity's sake — now, Lord, a few drops more on my vineyard — stop! — now give us a wee bit more sunshine!' — If you listen to them you would think prayer was a kind of whip with which to drive their Maker, as a gardener does his old ass that turns a water-wheel. The worst of all this is that they cannot agree among themselves; one wants wet weather, another dry, so they take refuge with the saints, for you must know that there are thirty-seven of them up there, who have charge of rainy weather. The foremost with his lance in his hand, is the great St. Médard. — The fair-weather saints are only two in number, St. Raymond and St. Dié, and it is their duty to brush away the clouds. Then there are St. Blaise, the wind calmer, St. Christopher, St. Valerian, and St. Aurelian who saves us from the hail, the storm, and the thunder; lastly, St. Clare who sweeps the cobwebs out of the sky. — The contradictory prayers of our farmers stir up discord in heaven, and all these saintly personages are at daggers drawn with one another, till Sts. Susan, Helen, and Scholastica actually pull each other's hair down. The good Lord himself does not know where to turn, and if He does not know, how is it with His poor vicar? After all it is none of my business; my duty is only to forward petitions and the Proprietor can attend to them as He sees fit. This idolatry positively revolts me, but I would not object if these good-for-nothings would not drag me into their quarrels with Heaven, but they are mad enough to try to make use of me and the Cross as a talisman against the pests which devour their crops. They wanted the rats driven away from the grain in their barns, so there were prayers, exorcisms, and processions in honor of St. Nicaise; — all this on a bitter day in December, with snow up to my neck; I have had lumbago ever since. Then caterpillars attacked them, and we had more processions, this time addressed to St. Gertrude, in a March storm with melting sleet; — a racking cough for me was the result. Now we have the locusts, and they want another procession round the orchards; think of it! with the sun like a furnace, and black clouds rolling up before a thunderstorm. I should come back with a rush of blood to the head, chanting the verse 'Ibi ceciderunt, workers of iniquity, atque expulsi sunt!' but it is I who would be cast out, — ('Sacred to the memory of Baptiste Chamaille, commonly called Dulcis, vicar of this parish.') — No! I am in no hurry to quit this world, and the best of jokes may be carried too far. It is no business of mine to get rid of their caterpillars, and as for their locusts, the lazybones can drive them off with their own hands. Help yourself and others will help you! It would be really too comfortable for them to sit down and let me do all the work. No, I will do my duty to the Lord, and let them do likewise. They can besiege me here if they choose. It would not bother me in the least, and I tell you, my friends, that they could raise this house from the ground easier than they could make me move out of this armchair. So now let's have another bottle." Having come to the end of his breath and his eloquence, he took a long drink and we followed his example, looking through our glasses at the world and our future which appeared rosy enough. Then there was silence for a few moments. — Each had his own special way of drinking, Paillard smacked his lips, looked at his glass inside and out, held it up to the light, tasted the wine and swallowed it down little by little, taking it in through his nose and his eyes as much as by his palate. Chamaille threw the wine into his big throat at one gulp. "Ha!" he would say as he felt it going down, rolling up his eyes to Heaven. As for me, I enjoyed both drink and drinkers; the more I looked at them the happier I felt. What can be more delightful than to taste two pleasures at once? All the same the bottle did not stand still with me. Not one of the three was behind the others, but would you believe it? at the end of the race the old notary was first by a good bumper. Our souls seemed to dilate under this refreshing dew, which moistened our throats and brightened up our wits and our faces. We leaned out of the open window, touched and charmed at the sight of the fields in their fresh spring dress, the young poplar shoots opening under the soft sunshine, the Yonne down in the valley twisting and turning through the meadows, like a playful puppy. We could hear the gay voices of women as they beat their linen on the stones, and the ducks quacking among the reeds. By this time Chamaille had quite recovered his good humor and began to talk as he leaned out between us. "It's a pretty good place to live in after all; we were all three of us born here, the Lord be praised! Was there ever a sweeter, dearer country? it fairly smiles at you, it is so soft, so tender and graceful, fit to bring tears to your eyes and to make your mouth water." We nodded our heads, and he began again. — "Our Master of course does what is right, we all know that, but why the devil did He put such disagreeable people in this heavenly place? I wish with all my heart that He would send them off somewhere to live under the Incas or the Great Mogul, anywhere but here." — "But, Chamaille," said we, "all men are alike, you would not gain by getting rid of these." — "Well then, they must have come into this world not that I might save their souls, but to discipline mine through this earthly Purgatory. My friends, you must admit that no lot is so hard as that of a country priest who has to struggle to knock the truths of our holy religion into the thick skulls of these stupid peasants; they may take in the Catechism with their mother's milk but it does not stay by them, for such rude natures need coarse provender. They will fill their mouths with aves and litanies, often just for the sake of hearing themselves; they will bray out vespers and complines, but the sacred words seldom get any farther than their thirsty jaws; for all the good done to their hearts and stomachs they might as well have held their tongues; pagans they were before, and pagans they remain. We have been striving for hundreds of years to drive out the gnomes and fairies from our fields, woods, and streams; but though we crack our cheeks and lungs in the effort to blow out these infernal fires, so that we can make God's true light to shine in the black darkness of the world, we cannot prevail over these base spirits, vulgar superstitions, of the earth earthy. The people will still find some of this brood of Satan hidden in the trunks of aged oaks, or under rocking stones, though the Lord alone knows how many we have broken, thrown down, and uprooted; but to get rid of all the devils which our mother Gaul holds hidden within her, would be endless. Every sod and stone in the country would have to be overturned. The truth is, nature is always slipping through our fingers; if you clip her wings one day they grow out the next, and ten gods spring up for each one that you destroy. Our stupid peasants think everything is a god or a devil; and they believe in were-wolves, headless horses, human snakes, imps, and sorcerers. Just imagine the figure the gentle Son of Mary and Joseph must cut among all these monsters out of Noah's ark!" — "If we could only see ourselves as others see us," said Paillard. "No doubt your people are a crazy lot, but how about you yourself? is there much to choose between you? and are your saints much better than demons and fairies? Three Gods in one was not enough; besides a goddess mother, you fill your Pantheon and the niches left empty by the old deities, with all kinds of godlings, male and female; but as far as I can see these newcomers are no better than the old: they appear like snails from no one knows where, deformed, maimed, eaten up with dirt and vermin. — They make a display of their sores and ulcers; one carries a trencher on his head, another sticks his head itself under his arm, like a hat. Then there is his saintship who goes about with his skin in his hand, and worst of all here in this Church is your own particular St. Simon Stylites, who stood for forty years on top of a pillar on one leg, for all the world like a crane."

"Hold up there!" cried Chamaille, jumping from his seat. "Say what you please about the other saints, they are no affair of mine, but here in St. Simon's own house, the least we can do is to be civil to him."

"Well, as I am your guest, I will leave your old crane in peace on his pedestal, but how about the Abbot of Cortigny who has the Blessed Virgin's milk in a bottle, and Count Sermizelles who took powdered relics and washed them down with holy water when he happened to need medicine?"

"You might do the same thing under the same circumstances," said Chamaille, "for all that you laugh at it now, — but as for the Abbot of Cortigny, or any other monk, they would sell angel's milk or archangel's cream, if they thought they could get our customers away from us: we are like cat and dog; their very name is an abomination to me!"

"Come, now, do you believe in these relics, or do you not?"

"I believe in my own, not in theirs, of course, — I have here the shoulder-blade of St. Diétrine, a sovereign cure for the scurvy, and the skull of St. Etoupe, which drives devils out of the sheep. — Now what are you jeering at? I tell you I have documents here, signed parchments, to prove the truth of what I say; if you do not believe me, I will go and fetch them."

"Sit down, old man, I don't want to see your documents; now, Chamaille, honor bright, you have no more faith in these things than I have, I can see it in your eye. A bone is a bone, no matter where it comes from, and you are an idolater if you adore it. Everything has its place in this world, and corpses should stay in the graveyard; so for my part I believe in life, in the light of day. I know that I live and think — very clearly too, — I know also that two and two make four, and that the earth is a fixed star hung in infinite space. — I believe in our local customs, and could recite the whole list of them to you. Then there are books where man's knowledge and experience are distilled drop by drop! I believe firmly in them. Above all I trust my own understanding, and like any wise and prudent man, I have faith in Holy Writ. Now are you satisfied?"

At this Chamaille fairly lost his temper. "What! satisfied?" cried he; "you are a horrible mixture of Calvinist, heretic, and Bible-pattering Huguenot; you would push aside even the vicar, and presume to dictate to your Mother Church. Oh! generation of vipers!"

It was now Paillard's turn to be angry, because, as he said, he could not suffer any one to apply the term Huguenot to him; he declared he was a loyal Frenchman and son of the Church, and had a good head on his shoulders too, so that he could see through a millstone as well as the next man; that he knew a fool when he saw him, and Chamaille was three parts a fool or three fools in one, just as he pleased; and he added that since God is the fountain of light and reason, if we would respect God, we should respect our own reason also.

After this silence settled down, except for an occasional grunt as they sat back to back at the table, finishing their bottle. —I burst out laughing, and they noticed then for the first time that I had taken no part in the dispute, though I had followed the whole argument with delight, and caught myself imitating the motions of their lips, frowning when they frowned, and moving my features like a rabbit eating a cabbage leaf. Now they both appealed to me to know on which side I was.

"I agree with both of you," said I, "and not with you alone: let us thresh this thing out together. Folly leads to laughter, and laughter to wisdom;—when you want to estimate your possessions what do you do? You begin naturally by writing down your column of figures, and then you add them up. Now why not pursue the same method with any crotchets you may have in your head? Add them all together and the sum may be a truth, though truth is hard to seize, and mocks at those who would lay hands on her; still there is more than one answer to the riddle of the world, my children. We only see one side of the shield, so I am for all gods, pagan and Christian alike, and for the god of reason first and foremost."

This lucid exposition had no better result than to unite both the others in an onslaught on me, and what they called my pagan and atheistic opinions. "Atheist!" cried I, "and why not? my door is open to all comers; gods and laws of every degree are welcome. I reverence God, and worship His saints, and love to gossip and laugh with such as are good company, but to tell you the plain truth, one god is not quite enough for a man as greedy as I am, so I have saints and saintesses, fairies and spirits of the earth, air, and water. I believe in reason, but I believe also in folly, from which truth sometimes springs. If I have faith in sorcery, I like also to think of this earth hanging in the clouds, and I should love to have my fingers on all the springs that move the world. —What joy to listen to the bright-eyed planets, and watch the man in the moon. — 'Silly talk! ' say you, who are all for rule and order, but let me tell you, these things are to be had at a price only, and a high one. To be orderly means not to follow one's own will, but that of others; it means to cut down the tall trees that the highroad may run straight;—convenient if you will, but ugly as the devil. No, mine are the old Gallic ideas,— many chiefs and a strong law, but every man for himself, and all brothers. Believe as you choose, but leave me to my belief, and the worship of my reason. Above all, let the gods alone; they are everywhere, in the heavens and in the waters under the earth; the world teems with them, and I not only respect those I know, but I am willing to accept new ones; only no one shall take from me one I have already known, unless he has deceived me."

Paillard and the vicar looked at me with positive compassion, and asked how I expected to get through the world with my head in such a tangle.

"There is no difficulty as to that," I assured them. "I know just where to put my feet. Do you think I need to take the highroad from Clamecy to Vézelay when I can cut through the woods? I find my way blindfold through little bypaths, it takes rather longer perhaps, but I pick up something for my game-bag. In my world everything is in its place: God in His Heaven, the saints in their chapels, out of doors the fairies, and my good brains in my head, so it all works smoothly; to each his proper task, with no despotic king to rule over us. It is more like a confederation of allied cantons, some strong and others weak; but in case of necessity the little ones band together, and who will get the upper hand then? Of course the Lord is mightier than any fairy, but it is another pair of shoes when a swarm of fairies make common cause against Him. The biter, you know, is sometimes bit. You think me crazy I know, but it sticks in my head that the head God of all is yet to be seen, for He is above everything; far, far away like our good King; we know his stewards and lieutenants only too well, but he is invisible in his palace, — so the sovereign to whom we bow is one Concini. Now, Chamaille, don't look at me like that, if you like it better, we will say that the Duke of Nevers is our ruler just now. Blessings on his head! I admire and respect him, but when he of the Louvre raises his voice our Duke is silent, and a good thing too!"

"I wish it were good," said Paillard, "but as the proverb says, when the sun is hid, you see the stars, and since the death of our lamented Henry, the whole kingdom is under petticoat government, princes and all; you know who profits by the sport of nobles; there are plenty to dip their fingers in the bag of gold, (the price of future triumphs,) that Sully has laid up there in the Arsenal. How long, O Lord? before these thieves are brought to justice!"

This was the signal for us to break out and talk with the utmost imprudence; for we had now hit on a tune which we could all sing, and we did sing it with variations on princes, hypocrites, lazy monks, and fat prelates. It is only fair to Chamaille to say that his improvisations on this theme were by far the most brilliant; but the trio continued in most melodious measure to chant of bitter and sweet, of those who have too much faith, and those who have none; fanatics, Huguenots, bigots, and fools who think that they can put the fear of God into a man by a dagger thrust or a blow on the head. As if we were donkeys to be driven with a stick along the heavenly way! Damnation should be free to all who desire it, but let them burn in a future state without tormenting them here on earth, and meanwhile leave us in peace, each to act as seems good in his own eyes. We are told that Christ died for men; for the infidel, as well as the Christian, and in truth are we not all poor creatures, as like as peas in a pod, neither better nor worse? What place, then, should pride and cruelty have among us?

Somewhat fatigued by all this conversation, we then resumed the worship of Bacchus, the only god respected by all three; even Chamaille declared that all the monks and sermons in the world could not turn him from this allegiance, for Bacchus is everywhere acknowledged as of true French lineage, and a real Christian. Are there not old pictures where our Saviour is represented treading the winepress under His feet? "Let us drink then, my friends, to our smiling god, whose red blood warms our hillsides and vineyards, rejoices our hearts, loosens our tongues, and breathes his right generous spirit over our France, filling her with the elixir of life."

Just here we stopped to take breath, and drink to France and common sense; for her motto is always to avoid extremes, if you would be wise; sometimes, it is true, one falls between two stools. All at once we heard a great banging of doors and heavy steps on the stairs, mingled with portentous puffings and appeals to all the saints in the calendar, and Mistress Louisa, the vicar's housekeeper, made her appearance, wiping her fat red face with a corner of her apron. "Oh! Master, you are wanted at once! Come and help us."

"Come where, you old fool?" said her master with pardonable irritation.

"Oh! save us, they will be here in a jiffy!"

"Who? the caterpillars? — let them spread over the fields. Now I won't hear another word about those brutes of farmers."

"But they are threatening the most dreadful things!"

"Pooh! what do I care for them? Do they threaten to bring me before the Tribunal? Let them come on, I am ready for them."

"Ah, dear Master! a suit is nothing to what they threaten to do."

"For the love of Heaven, woman, speak out!"

"They are all at big Picq's house down in the village, and what do you think? They are making charms and exorcisms to drive all the mice and insects from their own fields to your orchard and cellar!"

Chamaille sprang to his feet. "To think of those fiends! Sending locusts to eat up my fruit! How dare they even think of such a thing! St. Simon, have mercy on your poor vicar!"

We could not help laughing, and tried our best to calm him, but it was of no use.

"It is all very well!" he cried, "but you would laugh on the other side of your mouths if you were in my shoes; I suppose I must go and get my storeroom ready for these guests! Locusts! How revolting! And mice! It is enough to drive one crazy!"

I tried to persuade him that he could easily get the better of his parishioners and advised him to try some strong counter exorcism, but nothing could console him.

"I am lost!" he cried, wringing his hands. "Picq is terribly clever and sharp; the Lord alone knows what will come of it. I shall have to give in. To think how happy and comfortable I was just a minute ago! Ah! my dear friends, it is all up with me. Run, Louisa; run, and tell them to stop; say I am coming as fast as I can. Beasts that they are! Just let them wait till the next time they are dying and send for me! Well, the will of the Lord be done; it is not the first time I have had to knuckle down."

"Where are you going, old man?" we said.

"I am off on a crusade against locusts, of course!" he cried.

IV
The Idler

A Day in Spring.

FAIR April, daughter of spring, the pink and white apricot blossoms are like your slender breasts, and your sweet eyes shed soft sunshine over my garden. Ah! what a lovely day lies before me! And how good to stretch my old arms and shake off the stiffness of the night. I have been working hard for the last two weeks to make up for lost time, and we three, my two apprentices and I, have made the shavings fly under our planes, but unfortunately we rather lack customers; there are few to buy, and fewer still to pay for what they order; now purses are lean and empty, but red blood still runs in our arms, good soil is in our fields, and we reign over both.

Since early morning the voice of the working city has risen up to Heaven, "Our Father, give us our daily bread," but meanwhile, like sensible folks, we are kneading it ourselves... . You can hear the clatter of the millwheel, the wheeze of the forge bellows, and the hammers beating on the anvil; horses stamp and splash through the ford, carts bump along the road, whips crack, wooden shoes go pitter-patter; the butcher swings his chopper, the cobbler sings as he hammers in his nails,—and above is the blue spring sky, the white clouds flying before the light fresh breeze, and the genial sun warming everything. My youth revives, coming from far on swift wings to build her swallow's nest in my old heart once more, where she is more than ever welcome after her long absence, dearer even than in those first sweet days.

Just at this moment I hear the harsh grind of the weather-cock on the roof, or is it my old woman screaming something or other at me? I turn a deaf ear, but deuce take the sound, it has scared away my lovely youth... . She—I mean my wife—comes down in a rage as usual.

"What in the world are you doing there with your arms folded, gazing into the clouds, with your big mouth open as if you expected larks to drop into it? while here am I working for you like a pack-horse,— you think that's what women are made for, but the good Lord never meant Adam to stand with his hands in his pockets while his wife slaved about the house. I say he ought to take his share of all that is going, good and bad alike; there must be that much justice in Heaven or I will know the reason why! Stop laughing, you great fool! Get to work if you want to eat. Ah! I thought that would hit him! Now then begin, and the sooner the better."

"Of course I am going," said I, smiling sweetly. "It is a sin to stay in the house on a day like this." So back I went to the workshop and told my apprentices to come with me to Rion's woodyard to choose a long smooth plank for the work I had in hand. Cagnat, Robinet, and I went out whistling, and met my old girl on the threshold still railing at men and things.

"Don't go on so about it, Mistress," said Cagnat, "we shall be back in no time."

"I don't believe a word of it," shrieked my sweet partner.

Nine was striking on the town clock as we reached Béyant, no distance at all, but we had the manners to pause just a second at the bridge and speak to Fétu, Gadin, and Trinquet, who were sitting on the parapet watching the water — by way of beginning their working day. We had a moment's chat about nothing in particular, and then went on our way like steady responsible workmen, straight on, saying nothing to anybody, because, for one thing, there was no one on the road; but being persons of taste, we appreciated the beauties of nature, admiring the sky, the fresh spring verdure, a blooming apple-tree under the walls, the flight of a swallow, with some talk about the weather and the direction of the wind. All at once I remembered that I had not seen my little Glodie the whole morning, so I told my men to go on ahead, I would catch up with them at Rion's.

When I got to Martine's I found her down on her knees scrubbing the shop, her tongue going like a mill-race, talking to her husband, to his apprentice, to Glodie, to every one else within hearing, in the highest of spirits, and the floor being done, she flung the dirty water into the street, and hit me fair on the legs, where I was standing just outside the door admiring her, — there is no use denying it, she is the light of my eyes. Of course we both laughed louder than ever; she made a real picture, with her dark hair all tousled over her bright eyes and thick eyebrows, her lips as red as ripe plums, and her plump neck and arms, and her skirts tucked up just as far as need be.

"I hope you got it all, Father Noah?"

"Every drop, but I don't mind that, as long as I am not obliged to drink it."

In I went and kissed my little Glodie, who was sitting under the counter to be out of the wet.

"I bet I know what brought you here so early in the morning," said Martine.

"You knew the reason before you were born," was my answer.

"You mean Mother?"

"Who else?"

"Men are such cowards!"

Florimond heard the last word, just as he was coming in, and drew himself up, thinking it was meant for him. "No offense," said I, "she was talking to me."

"If the cap fits put it on!" said my daughter.

Florimond always stands a good deal on his dignity and hates to be laughed at; besides he is apt to be suspicious of Martine and me when we get together, and fancies, sometimes with some reason, that we are making him the butt of our jokes, so I said innocently, "You know well enough, Martine, that Florimond is master in his own house, not like your poor old father, who always let himself be put upon; you inherit your docile submissive nature from me, my child."

"Get along with you, old humbug," cried Martine, who by this time was at her house-cleaning again, rubbing the windows, the walls, and the furniture, as if to take the very skin off. She filled the whole place to overflowing with life and energy, while in the background stood Florimond as usual, stiff and particular; he is always chilly, never quite at his ease with us, our jokes shock him, and he cannot understand why we often laugh just out of sheer health and jollity, for he is himself somewhat undersized, thin, and low-spirited. Nothing is ever quite to his mind, perhaps because he is always thinking of himself, so there he stood with a knitted scarf round his scraggy fowl's neck, and kept glancing about uneasily, till at last he said:

"There is a gale here fit to blow your head off. Shut a few of those windows."

"It is as hot as Tophet!" said Martine, scrubbing harder than ever, but as a matter of fact there was a good fresh breeze coming in from all directions, too much for Florimond, who went off like a thunder-cloud. "He can go back and warm himself in his oven," she said, laughing. I could not help asking her how she got along with her baker, though I knew perfectly well she would let herself be cut in pieces before she would admit that she had ever made a mistake; true enough, she declared that he suited her down to the ground. "One should always be content with what one has," said she.

"You are right," said I, "but if I may venture to say so, I should think your little man might sometimes have cause for uneasiness."

"And why, I should like to know? My worst enemy would admit that I am a woman of my word, if he keeps his part of the bargain, but if he doesn't, just let him look out for himself, that's all I have to say. If he does his duty, I will do mine!"

"His whole duty?"

"You don't suppose he would admit that it is too much for him?"

Martine sat back on her heels, her bright eyes sparkling with laughter, then jumped up and gave me a great push.

"You are wasting my whole day for me, there never was such an old gossip since the world was made. Get out now, take Glodie with you, she is forever under my feet, with her fingers in everything that goes on, (there, she has been in the bakeshop again, I can see dough on her nose). Get along with you, do, before I sweep you both out!"

So out we had to go, glad enough to be together, and on the way at last to Rion's, but there were some fishermen by the riverside, and we had to stop to look at them, give them some advice and watch the line, and see the float disappear under the green water with a jerk. Glodie noticed the worm wriggling on the hook. "Poor thing," she said, "he is going to be eaten, and that makes him unhappy."

"Well, darling, it is rather nasty to be eaten, but then think how nice for the fish that swallows him, and says, 'that's good!'"

"How would you like it, Grandad, if any one swallowed you?"

"I should say, 'What luck for the man that gets such a toothsome morsel!' It is just the way you look at it, ducky, everything is good if you only see it in the right light; all is for the best to a true son of Burgundy."

It was not quite eleven o'clock when we got to Rion's, and there we saw Binet, (who like a careful lad had brought his rod), fishing for gudgeon, while Cagnat lay stretched out on the grass looking on.

I went on to the woodyard, for there is nothing I love so well as to handle the big logs stripped of their bark, and breathe in the clean fresh smell of sawdust; on my honor I believe a fine tree appeals to me even more than a woman, though I am not one of those narrow fools who can only enjoy one thing at a time. If I were in the slave market at Constantinople, and saw the girl of my heart there among twenty other beauties, do you think my love for her would prevent me from seeing the charms of the others? No, thank Heaven! my eyes are windows wide open to beauty of every kind, and nothing is lost on me. I am besides rather a sharp old bird, — long experience, you know, — and can detect the little tricks and dodges of the fair sex under no matter what disguise; in the same way beneath the rough skin of my tree-loves I can see life waiting for me to bring it forth.

Meanwhile Cagnat (who is impatient, like all young men) has been exchanging pleasantries at the top of his voice with loungers on the other end of the bridge, for though the people in the two suburbs may differ in some ways, they both like to spend the livelong day sitting on the wall of the bridge, with occasional trips to the nearest tavern; and as you may guess, a conversation between Beuvron and Béyant consists chiefly of abuse. They call us Burgundy snails and peasants; we retort with "frogs," or "pike-eaters," —I say "we," because for the life of me, I never can keep out of any squabble that's going on; it seems just ordinary civility to answer when you are spoken to. In the midst of our little encounter, all at once the clock struck twelve! Noon already? There must be something wrong with the hourglass, still I ought to be getting home, so I pressed our friends, who were looking on, to help us load our planks on the cart, and give us a hand with it back to Beuvron. "Cheeky devil," was their first answer, but at bottom they were good-natured enough, so off we went running up the hill to the admiration of all beholders. When we got to our own bridge there were Fétu, Gadin, and Trinquet, just where we left them three hours ago, still watching the water. They jeered at us for working so hard, we called them good-for-nothings, and as the issue seemed in doubt, I sat down on the corner to see how it would all turn out, when suddenly I heard a well-known voice, and there was the old lady, "Will you tell me what you have been doing with yourself ever since nine this morning? It is my belief that you would never come home, if I did not drag you in by the hair of your head, idle, greedy vagabond! And your dinner is all burnt to a cinder!"

"You win!" said I, laughing; "there's not one of these boys that can stand up to you when it comes to talking—but I was on my way home truly. I had only stopped to rest,—go ahead, I'll be there in a minute."

The two apprentices, my wife, and Glodie went off towards home at a brisk pace, and I followed in a more leisurely manner—I was going as I was bid, when down from the upper town came the sound of voices, of horns, and the gay chimes from St. Martin's tower; and I remembered that the wedding of Mademoiselle Lucretia Champeaux, and Monsieur d'Amazy, the Receiver of Taxes, was to take place today. Every one made a bee-line for the castle, and rushed off at the top of his speed, I among the foremost, for shows like that don't come our way often. Fétu, Gadin, and Trinquet were the only ones who stayed behind, as if they were glued to the wall of the bridge; they said it was undignified to put themselves out for those upper-towners, and as a rule I agree with them, and stand on my dignity as much as any man, but not when it comes between me and my amusement,—there is reason in all things! I took the flight of thirty-six steps up to St. Martin's at one jump, but all the same by ill-luck I was not in time to see the wedding procession, which had already gone into church; naturally there was nothing left for me to do but to wait and see it come out, but as the service seemed interminably long—the clergy love the sound of their own voices,—I managed to squeeze my way between the bulging corporations of my fellow-citizens, till I found myself just inside the door under a regular human feather-bed. I am the last man to forget the respect due to the sacred edifice otherwise I might have been up to some of my jokes, but I know what's what, and can be solemn as an owl at the right moment. Only sometimes even owls lose their gravity, and that is what happened to me, for while I was standing there, a model of propriety and devotion, the service went on, and as Monsieur d'Amazy is a great votary of the chase, hunting-horns were introduced at suitable moments. If only the pack of hounds had been there too! I did not dare to laugh, of course, but I whistled a flourish under my breath, and just then came the crucial point of the ceremony when the bride answers "Yes "to the fatal question. At once the horns burst out with the "set to," and that was too much for me; I cried, "Hallali!" and the whole church roared with laughter, so that the beadle came to restore order, and I thought it a good time to make my way out, as quiet as a mouse.

There were plenty of people outside, many like myself who are aware that ears were made to hear, eyes to see, and tongues to tell what takes place — or what does not, — in the world around us; so it seemed but a moment before the great doors swung open again, and the sound of the organ came pouring out, as the bridal party appeared. First came the Amazy, leading his beautiful prize, her large eyes glancing to right and left like a frightened doe as she advanced. Lovely creature! I wish she had fallen to my charge, but to whom much is given, of him much is demanded, and Amazy has his work cut out for him. Unfortunately I saw little more, so that afterwards I could not even describe the dresses of the bride and bridegroom, for just then we were distracted by a grave question of precedence which arose among the dignitaries who formed part of the procession.

I shall never get over having missed the entrance into the church, for it seems that the Chief Magistrate of the Manor, and the Provost, acting as Mayor, had locked horns in the doorway like two old rams, and the Mayor being the bigger man got through first; the great question now was which of the two would be first coming out, so bets were freely offered, and meanwhile the head of the procession went on its way, but the tail delayed its appearance. We could see, just inside the entrance, that a furious dispute was in progress between the rival officials, and as they could not talk loud in church, there they were, scolding, puckering their faces into the most portentous frowns and scowls, and cursing at each other, all in dumb show. It was enough to make one die of laughing, but we all ended by taking part with one side or the other; the older ones for the Judge, because he was the Duke's representative, and you must respect others, if you would be respected yourself; but the young men inclined to the side of the Mayor as champion of our liberties, and personally I backed the better man. We all shouted to encourage them with cries of "Go it, Grasset!" — "At him again, Pétaud!!" — "Shut his mouth!" But to our great disappointment the contestants were too much afraid of spoiling their fine clothes to get to their hands, and the dispute might have lasted till the crack of doom, — for there was no danger of their breath giving out, — if it had not been for the priest, who wanted to get to the castle in time for dinner, — so he smoothed them down, telling them it was bad manners to be late, and worse yet to show their evil tempers in the house of the Lord, that they could settle their difficulties another time, — and in short he got them all in motion. I was not near enough to hear all this, but I could see that he put his two big hands behind their heads and brought their faces gently together for the kiss of peace, and out they all came at last, marching in two lines, with the big priest in the middle. When masters fall out, we are always the gainers, so we were well pleased to see three at the head of the column, instead of one.

When they had all gone into the castle where their well-earned feast awaited them, we remained outside sniffing the delicious odors of a dinner we were not to share; but it was a sort of satisfaction to hear the list of dishes, for there were three of us there, Tripet, Bauldequin and I, who knew what was good, so our mouths watered as we heard all the toothsome things, and we approved or not as seemed best to us, the final decision being that the dinner was not so bad on the whole, only we ought to have been consulted, as persons of experience. When jugged hare was mentioned, every one had his own recipe to give, — for by this time we had a circle of auditors, — and there was lively disputing to and fro, in which I took part, as I always maintain that a man who is not interested in such subjects is nothing but a fish.

The best housekeepers in the town are Mistresses Perrine and Jacquette, who are rivals in the art of dinner-giving; each tries to eclipse the other, and naturally each has her partisans, for our best jousts in Clamecy take place at table. No one loves a good argument better than I do, but I would rather be doing myself than hear the exploits of others, and I cannot grow fat by talking of other men's dinners. Tripet was of my way of thinking, and you may guess that I was delighted when he whispered to me:

"It is ill talking of good drink to the thirsty, or of love to a neglected lover; I can't stand any more of this sort of thing; it is as if a beast were gnawing at my vitals; let us find some place where we can feed him."

I told him to come along with me, that I knew where to look for the best remedy for his complaint; of course neither of us thought for a moment of going home, it was after two o'clock, and we should have found tempers boiling and soup cold, so we made for the Dolphin Inn at the corner of the High Street. It was market day, so the room was crowded, but we managed to get a table, and after all nothing is so appetizing as to see one's friends around one, unless it be to sit down all alone to a good meal, — both ways are best.

For some time we had better use for our jaws than to talk. A delicate little shoulder of lamb with cabbage fully occupied us; on top of that a pint of the best, just to clear the mist from our eyes, — you know the proverb, "To eat dry, blinds the eye. Food unwined makes a man blind," but when we had washed the dust out of our throats we had time to look about and enjoy ourselves. At the next table sat a vicar from the country and an old woman, a farmer's wife, full of respect for his Reverence, bowing and bending her old head and turning up her eyes as if in the confessional; and he too had something of the same air, sitting sidewise, returning bow for bow, but with his mouth full, radiating forgiveness of sins from a full stomach.

Further on was our notary, Pierre Delavau, who was treating a brother lawyer to a good solid meal. The air was thick around them with talk of interest, money, politics, contracts—Roman republics, etc., for he likes to dabble in such things on a holiday, but in everyday life is a conservative loyal subject of the King.

My eye lighted presently on Perrin Le Queux, who caught sight of me at the same moment, and waved his glass towards me with the greatest cordiality,—old fox, in his stiff starched blouse! I'll bet he saw me the moment I came in, but as he owes me the price of a fine carved oak chest for the last two years, he was conveniently short of sight. He jumped up and came over to our table.

"The best of luck!" said he, holding out his bottle, and when I shook my head he still pressed it on me. "At least you will have a bite of dinner," he said, thinking of course I would refuse, having already dined, but I took him up at once. "So much to the good on my bill," thought I to myself.

We began all over again, but this time without undue haste, as the first rage of hunger was abated and the crowd thinning out,—there are always people who leave as soon as they have swallowed their food,—and there remained only men of ripe age and wisdom who know what's what, and reckon a good dish to be equal to a good deed any day. I sat where I could feel the sunshine and fresh air through the open door, where some chickens were picking at the crumbs, and an old hound lay dozing on the threshold; outside were the street cries, "Fine fish!"—"Mend your windows!" and the shrill voices of women. On the other side of the dusty square were two big white oxen lying down with their legs folded under them, peacefully chewing the cud, with their eyes half shut, while from the sunny roofs came the cooing of pigeons. Really I could have cooed or purred myself if any one had stroked my back. We all began to talk from table to table, in perfect good-fellowship, the country vicar, the notary, his partner, the innkeeper (Baiselat by name), and I, and as we were all full, and contented with our lot, we took a certain pleasure in discussing the hard times and the political situation. We all groaned over the bad state of business, the high cost of living, the poverty and ruin of France, general decadence of the race, mistakes in administration, etc., but we were careful to name no names, for the ears of the great are as large as their fortunes, and who knows when an unlucky word may drop into them? Truth, as we know, is at the bottom of a well, so we ran but little risk in abusing those of our masters who were the farthest off, especially that wretched Concini brought from Florence under the fat Queen's petticoats. Each had something to say against him, and with perfect justice, for if you catch two curs fighting over a bone, you beat your own dog, of course, but you half kill the stranger. However, I took the other side of the argument, partly for love of fair play, and partly out of perversity; so I said the dogs should be treated alike, that any one would suppose, to hear people talk, that all our evils were imported from Italy, whereas if the truth were known plenty of wicked things, and wicked people too, grow in our own garden. To this they all declared with one voice that a scamp from over the Alps was three times worse than one of us, and that three honest Italians were not equal to a third of a good Frenchman. I answered that man is pretty much the same animal wherever you find him, that I knew a good one when I saw him, and liked him, even if he came out of Italy, but this raised a perfect riot, and they all fell on me at once saying they knew I talked like that because I was a wanderer and a gadabout, always stumping along the highroad. I had to admit that there was some truth in this, for in my time I did kick about the world a good deal, when our good lord the old Duke—father of the present man—sent me to Mantua to study the enamels, potteries, and art industries which were afterwards transplanted here. The whole journey from St. Martin's to St. Andrew's in Mantua was made on my two feet, with a stick in my hand, so you may guess if I spared shoe-leather! I love to feel the ground under me, and the world before me where to choose, but don't say another word about it, or I shall be off again, like a true son of those Gauls who pillaged the world. "I should like to know what you ever brought back from your travels by way of booty," they said. As much as any of my ancestors; all that I could cram into my head or my eyes,—empty pockets if you like, but Lord! what a lot I saw and heard and tasted,—it is a treat only to think of it. A man cannot know all and see all, but he can do his best, and I was like a big sponge in the ocean, or rather like a ripe bunch of grapes full to bursting of the rich juices of the earth; you would have a fine vintage if you could squeeze me, but I mean to keep it for my own partioular drinking; you fellows pretend to look down on it, so much the better for me. When I first came home you know I tried to share some of my good things with you, the treasures I had picked up in sunny climes, but people here have no curiosity except about the doings of their neighbors; the rest of the world seems too far off, there is as good at home, and they think those who come from Rome are none the better for their journey. I never try to force a thing down any man's throat, so I kept what I had for myself, and let people go on in their own way, and I even went along with them, for that is the path of wisdom; you can't make people happy against the grain, but you can share content with them.

Following this plan I joined in the usual hymn of praise. What pride, what joy to be a Clamecyan! and I believe it, by Heavens! so I sat there furtively drawing Delavau's nose, and the curate's long arms which he flaps about when he speaks, and we talked about our good town;—a place where I was born must have merit,—besides, all human plants flourish here, they are not thorny and spiteful, even if their tongues are somewhat long and sharp at the end. No one is the worse for a little gossip, particularly if you get as good as you send; at bottom you love your neighbor as yourself, and would not hurt a hair of his head.

We are all proud of our province, which remained calm in the midst of the excitement everywhere else; our Provost Ragon would not join the Guisards, the League, the heretics, the Catholics, or any of the extremists, persecutors, or rebels; and it was here that St. Bartholomew came to wash his bloody hands, where we all stood firm around our good Duke, like an island of safety against which the waves of trouble dashed themselves in vain. — I cannot speak without emotion of Duke Louis, and our late King, — how we loved them both! — for we really seemed made for one another, in spite of faults on both sides; no one is perfect in this world, of course, but these very faults in them were endearing, and brought us closer together; they were so human! We used to laugh and say, "Nevers is younger than ever," or "Our good King is once more a father to his people!" Those were the good times, and we can truly say that we had the cream of it then — Delavau knew Duke Louis as well as I, but the honor of having seen King Henry is mine alone, and I love to tell for the hundredth time of how it happened. It always seems a new story to me and to my friends too, for they are Frenchmen of the right sort, and so I told them once more of the gray King mounted on a gray horse with his gray hat, his gray coat, — his elbows sticking through the sleeves, — his gray eyes, the outside all gray, but pure gold within!

Just as I was in the middle of my story the notary's clerk ran in to call him to a dying client, so I was interrupted, for he had to leave at once, which was all the more annoying as he had a story of his own on the tip of his tongue. I knew he had been hatching it for an hour, but I wanted first to get off my own little tale. I must admit in all fairness that his was funny when it did come; he has not his equal for a story with a dash of salt to it.

We all went out together, cheered from head to foot. It must have been just about five o'clock or a bit later, and see how in three short hours I had raked in two good dinners, and an order from the notary for an oak press, to say nothing of all the fun we had had going over old stories: — well, we just stopped to take a thimble full of cherry brandy and a biscuit at Rathery's, the apothecary, and then the party broke up. Delavau had finished one story and begun another, so as we wanted to hear the end of it, we went on with him as far as Mirandole, and there we left him at last, only stopping to lean against the wall for a minute or two, long enough to say good-by.

It was now rather too late to go home, or perhaps I should say too early, so I walked down towards Béyant with a man who was pushing his barrow loaded with charcoal, trumpeting his wares as he went. On the way we met a blacksmith coming up trundling a wheel before him;

when it slackened speed he made a running jump and sent it flying on ahead, for all the world like those allegories where you see men pursue Fortune which always eludes their outstretched hand. This impressed me as a very good image, and I made a note of it for future reference. I was in two minds which way to take towards home, when I saw a funeral issuing out of the hospital gates. First came two tiny choir-boys, giggling together as they walked, one carrying a cross three times as high as himself clutched against his little fat tummy. Behind came the body under its pall, borne by four tottering old men, and then the vicar. I felt it a matter of simple politeness to go with the poor sleeper to his last lodging, for misery loves company, and then I wanted to hear what the widow had to say. As is the custom, she was walking beside the officiating priest pouring out her sad tale; how the departed was taken ill, what remedies were applied, how he died, his faults, his virtues, his affection, in short the story of his life and hers, while the priest's chants filled in the pauses. Before we had gone far our numbers were swelled by many worthy souls with ears to hear and hearts to feel, so at last we came to the resting-place where they put down the bier at the edge of the grave. You know a pauper cannot take his wooden shirt with him — not that he sleeps the less sound for that, — so they lifted the pall and the coffin lid, and let him slide down into his hole. I threw a handful of earth over him, and made the sign of the Cross, to keep bad dreams away, and then went off at peace with all the world; since morning I had seen and heard everything, rejoiced with the fortunate, and wept with the sorrowful. My cup was full, and, the day being over, I sauntered back along the water-side.

I was making for the junction of the two rivers, meaning to follow the Beuvron to my own house, but the lovely evening tempted me on till almost without knowing it I found myself outside the town and I kept on by the bewitching little Yonne nearly to the narrows at La Forêt. The water flowed by calm and still with scarcely a ripple on its smooth surface; my sight was drowned in it, as a fish is held by the hook; the whole sky was entangled by the river as if in a net, where it seemed to float with its rosy clouds caught among the reeds and grasses, and the golden sun rays trailing in the water. There was an old cowherd on the bank with his two skinny cows: I went and sat down beside him, and as he was rather shaky on his pins, I told him of a remedy for his rheumatic complaint; — (I am rather a good doctor when I have time for it), — so he told me all about himself, his ills and sorrows, but he seemed jolly enough, and even resented my thinking him younger than he was. He was seventy-five years old, and took pride in it, saying the older you were, the more you could bear. It seemed quite right to him that we should all have to suffer, and, on the other hand, he said God's favors fall alike on the just and the unjust, so all is as it should be; rich and poor, gentle and simple will sleep at last in the same Father's arms.

As he talked his quavering old voice mingled with the chirp of crickets, the water pouring over the dam, the smell of wood and tar blowing towards us from the harbor, the tranquil flowing river, the fair reflections all melting into the peaceful evening.

When he had gone I walked back alone with my hands behind my back, watching the circles in the water, and was so absorbed that I forgot where I was till I heard a well-known voice on the other bank, and saw I was just opposite our house. There was my wife,—gentle soul!—shaking her fist at me out of the window! I fixed my eyes on the stream and made believe not to see her, but she was reflected upside down as if in a glass; I did not say a word, but shook all over with inward laughter, and the more I laughed the angrier she got. It was too killing to see her bobbing up and down in the Beuvron head first! At last she lost all patience; I heard doors and windows banging behind her, and she came rushing out after me like a whirlwind. She had to cross a bridge to get at me, and the question was which? Right or left, for we were just between the two. She made for the little footbridge to the right, and I naturally took the other, where I found Gadin planted on the very same spot where I had left him in the morning.

Night was falling as I came to my own door. Though I am not like that lazy Roman who was always complaining that he had lost a day, still I do not know where time goes, though none of this day has been lost, and I am content enough, but if only there were forty-eight hours instead of twenty-four! I do not feel that I always get my money's worth, for my glass is no sooner filled than it is empty; there must be a crack in it. I sometimes think I envy people who sip and sip without ever coming to the bottom. It cannot be that their glass is longer than mine, that would be too much to bear. "Hi there! you landlord of the Sun, fill up my mug to the brim when you are pouring out the daylight!" But I have nothing really to complain of, for the Lord has blessed me with an appetite that nothing can ever satisfy, so I love both day and night and cannot get enough of either.

Swift flying day of April, are you gone indeed? But it is good to feel that I have not lost a moment of your sweet presence. I have kissed and held you close in my arms;—so now welcome, dear night, it is your turn to share my couch, but good Lord! I forgot, there will be three of us, for the old woman is just coming up to look for me.

V
Belette

May.

THREE months ago I got an order from the château of Asnois for a dresser and a chest, but I would not begin to work on them until I was able to see the room and the place where they were to stand; for according to my idea, furniture is like wall fruit. A good apple comes from a good tree; and there is no use in telling me that a beautiful thing is beautiful no matter where it is, like a wayside Venus, who sells herself to the highest bidder. True art is an expression of our inmost selves; it is the spirit of home and of the fireside, our domestic deity; and to know him you must know the house where he dwells. He is so made for man, and his work meant to fulfil and complete man's existence, that nothing can be really beautiful unless it is in its proper setting.

I set off early, then, to see where my chest was to stand, and what with the walk and my dinner, it took up nearly half a day; but man must eat to live, and everything was so much to my mind, that I was in the best of spirits when I at last started back towards home. The path to Clamecy ran straight enough, but when I came to the crossroads, I could not help glancing down a by-way, which went wandering across the meadows, between the blossoming hedges.

Said I to myself, "How nice it would be to leave the stupid highroad, and follow that little path; the day is yet young, and anyhow it would never do to get home ahead of the sun, and early or late the wife will have something to say to me. ... I really must go a step or two farther, and have a look at that dear little pear tree; surely those are not snowflakes? no, of course not, they are the white petals blown off by the wind. Listen to the birds! and the tinkling of the brook, sliding along under the grass, like a kitten chasing a ball. ... I have a great mind to follow it, and see if the roots of this oak will not stop it; where can it have gone? well, upon my word! it has squeezed its way under the big gouty knees of yonder elm,—did you ever see such impudence? I might as well go and find out where this path does lead."

It was all very well to saunter along thus at the heels of my vagrant shadow, but in the back of my head I knew perfectly well where that beguiling footway would take me. Like Ulysses, I tried to play the hypocrite with myself, but the truth is, that I made up my mind where I meant to go from the moment I left the gates of Asnois. An old flame of mine lived at a mill down in these parts, and I had a fancy to go and surprise her,—or perhaps surprise myself, who knows? It was many a long day since I had set eyes on Céline, or "Belette" as they called her, and the chances were that her saucy face would be changed out of knowledge. Ah! Belette, I am not afraid of you now! Those little teeth of yours can no longer hurt this poor old dried-up heart! Perhaps the teeth are gone too? I can see them now, and hear your charming laughter! What a fool she did make of you, Breugnon; you were a mere toy in those hands of hers; but, after all, why not? if she could get some fun out of such a country blockhead as I was then. I learned the noble art of wood-carving from Master Médard Lagneau, and I can see myself now leaning over the wall of his place, gazing with my mouth open. The wall ran between the yard where we worked and a big kitchen garden, planted with lettuce, strawberries, pink radishes, cucumbers, and melons; and there, at all hours of the day, I could see a tall active slip of a girl, balancing two great watering pots in her strong brown hands, as she carefully sprinkled the thirsty borders. She wore a coarse chemise of unbleached linen, which showed her bare arms and long throat; her feet too were bare, and her short skirt was tucked up to her knees, which were round and strong like a boy's. The first thing you noticed about her was the heavy mass of her twisted reddish hair. I literally could not take my eyes off her as she came and went emptying her watering pots, going back to fill them at the well, carrying them steadily and carefully along the narrow paths, where her long bare toes felt their own way cleverly in the damp earth between the strawberry plants. She did not seem to know that I was there, keeping steadily on with her work; but when she came close, all at once she turned her head and shot a look at me. Ouch!—I can still feel the hook in my gills, and the net around me. "A woman's eye catches the fly," as the proverb has it. I struggled of course, but what was the use? There was the silly fly on the wall, with his wings stuck together.

She paid no more attention to me, and squatted down on her heels to plant her cabbage, but from time to time she stole a look to make sure that her prey was still there. There was no use in my saying to myself, "She is trying to make a fool of you, my lad!" I could see her snickering, and that made me grin too:—what an ass I must have looked! At last up she jumped, ran across the garden, came back, stuck her feet wide apart over the edge of the border, caught at a floating spray of bloom, and said, waving her arm at me, "Another good fellow gone!" As she spoke she thrust her flower in the front of her dress. "That's where I should like to be," said I, for though I may have been a fool at that age, I was no laggard in an affair of this kind.

She put her arms akimbo and burst out laughing. "Not for the likes of you," cried she. "Greedy!" ... That was the beginning of my acquaintance with the pretty gardener Belette, on a warm August evening.

The nickname of "Weasel "suited her long body, with the small head and pointed nose, and wide prominent mouth; just the mouth to crack nuts and hearts, and made too for laughter. Oh, her eyes! dark blue like thunder-clouds, and her wildcat smiling lips! — What chance had the poor prey, once in her toils?

I did very little work after this, but spent most of my time gawking over the wall, till Master Lagneau would come behind, and dislodge me with a vigorous kick. Belette got tired of me sometimes, and would tell me to stop staring at her and get out; but I often told her, with a wink, that you cannot know either a woman or a melon just by looking. How much I should have liked to try a slice of her! But perhaps another fruit would have served my turn then equally well; for I was at the age when a man could fall in love with the eleven thousand virgins. Did I love Belette really? — there are times when a boy like me will love anybody; — but no, Breugnon, that is all humbug, and you know it; your first love is the real article, your fate, marked out for you by the stars in their courses, and it is perhaps because I missed my destiny that my whole life long I have gone unsatisfied.

We understood one another at half a word; though we did nothing but tease. Both of us had glib tongues, and I would give her back as good as she sent, quick as lightning. Sometimes we nearly died of laughing, and when she thought that she had got the better of me, she would throw herself down and roll over and over on the ground with joy, among her beets and onions. She would come too and stand under my wall, and talk to me in the warm twilight evenings. How well I remember her once, as she stood there laughing, her bright eyes looking into mine, — she could see my heart at the bottom of them, — and I can see her now, as she reached up and pulled down a branch of the cherry tree, the ripe fruit resting like jewels on her hair, and then she did not pick the cherries, she just bit off the flesh of them, leaving the stones on the stem. Ah! eternal eager youth, with your lips at the fountain! — When I have been carving on a panel, how many a time since have I drawn the lines of her beautiful arms, her breast, her throat with the head thrown back, her full rich mouth! ... I bent over the wall, and drew the branch towards me, putting the moist stones to my lips, where I could still feel the touch of hers.

On Sundays we walked over to Beaugy, and there we used to dance; though I was a perfect stick at it in spite of what they say, that love lends wings, and would give grace to the very bean-poles. She was always at me, and never for a moment did we cease our sparring; she liked to laugh at my long crooked nose, my big mouth like an oven, my scrubby beard, and all the rest of it. They say we are made in the likeness of God, but I hope not, for His sake... . Belette at least never stopped laughing at my queer looks, and I did my best to get even.

This kind of thing went on till we both of us took fire. I shall never forget the vintage that year; Belette and I worked side by side, bent double among the poles, our heads nearly touching, and sometimes as I stripped the vines my hand would brush against her, and then she would rear up like a young colt and give me a smart slap, or squeeze a bunch of grapes in my face. Naturally I retorted with another, till the red juice ran down over her sunburned bosom. You never saw such a little devil as she was, but I could not catch her off her guard. We always kept a wary eye on each other, for she knew well enough what I was after; but she always seemed to be saying, "Don't you wish you may get it?" On my side, I was just like a cat with his eyes half shut, watching a mouse and ready to pounce at the right moment. "Wait till I catch you, my lady!" I thought.

One afternoon in this very month of May, — our summers must have been hotter in those days, — the air was like an oven, a furnace seven times heated; for hours black threatening clouds had been coming up, big with the storm which still held off, so that we melted under the heat, and the very tools stuck to our fingers. Belette had been singing in her garden, but after a while I could neither see nor hear her, till at last I caught sight of her sitting on a stone under the shed roof, asleep; her lips parted, her head leaning back against the doorpost, one arm resting on the big water-can, as if she were overcome by sudden lassitude. There she lay, half exposed, defenseless like Danaë, and I her Jupiter! — I dropped over the wall, crushing the cabbages and lettuce in my haste, and took her in my arms, putting my mouth to hers. How sweet she was! all warm and half-asleep! She seemed to yield, and returned my kisses, but without opening her blue eyes. — My blood burned in my veins, and I strained her to my breast with delight; at last, the ripe fruit had dropped into my longing mouth! — but in spite of my joy, some strange scruple now restrained me; I don't know what queer notions held me back, — great fool that I was! — but I felt that I loved her too much, — I could not take advantage of her so, — half asleep, not knowing what she did. My proud beauty! I would not have her unconsenting, and so, — I tore myself away from my happiness, untwining our linked arms and our lips, not without trouble, for man is fire, and woman tow: but I left her trembling, like that other simpleton you have heard of, who conquered Antiope. I too conquered, that is, I took to my heels: — I fairly blush when I think of it, at thirty-five years' distance. Foolish boy! yes, but what would I not give to be capable now of such folly? From that time Belette treated me as if she were possessed of the devil, never twice was she in the same mind; one day she would launch some insult at me, or ignore my very existence, and the next she would meet me with languishing sheep's eyes, and cajoling laughter. When my back was turned, she would hide behind a tree, and hurl lumps of sod at my neck, or hit me on the nose with a plum; and worse than all were her goings on with any man that she could pick up, when we were out on

Sundays. She took it into her head,—chiefly to annoy me, I do believe,—to flirt with Quiriace Pinon, a great chum of mine. He and I were like Orestes and Pylades, you never saw one without the other, and wherever there was anything going on, a fair, a fight, or a wedding, there we were in the midst of it. He was short and thickset, as sturdy as an oak, a good straightforward worker, and as for friendship! it would have gone hard with any one who interfered with me when he was by.

Belette singled him out from all the rest of her admirers, knowing well enough what it would mean to me; and she had no trouble at all with him, you may be sure.—A few smiles and glances out of those eyes of hers were quite enough to do his business. What son of Adam can resist the wiles of these serpents? She would put on her innocent unconscious air, turn her long neck and glance at him under her fringed eyelashes, flash her white teeth, lick her red lips with her little pointed tongue, then walk away, her whole supple body swaying as she moved.

Pinon lost his head completely, and so Belette soon had the two of us stuck up on the wall, watching her every step. She drew us both on, so it was not long before we were ready to fly at each other's throats; but when she thought the thing had gone far enough, she would throw a little cold water on the pair of us. Much as this last trick angered me, I could not help laughing at her, clever little cat! but it drove Pinon half out of his wits;—(a joke was always a sealed book to him, but he would roar at one that no one else could make head or tail of.)—When she was cold to him, he would lose his temper, stamp and swear at her like a madman, and she rather liked this rough sort of wooing, so different from my way with her.

She and I were really of the same Gallic breed—there was much more affinity between us than there was between her and Pinon, who was simply a ramping, stamping sort of a brute; but from pure caprice, or perhaps to vex me, she showed him the greatest favor, smiling at him with lips and eyes full of the sweetest promises; but when it came to keeping them, and he was ready to burst with pride in his conquest, then she would turn and march off, leaving him in the lurch.

All this was droll enough to me, but Pinon could not see the joke, and would turn on me like a tiger, because, forsooth! I was taking his girl away from him! It came to such a pass, that he actually told me to take myself out of the way; I replied that the very same words had been on the tip of my tongue.

"Well then, I shall have to punch your head for you!"

"It may come to that," said I, "but I should hate to do it."

"Me too," said he. "Now, Breugnon, one cock is enough in a farm-yard; do you get out of this, like a sensible fellow."

"By all means," said I, "only you are the one to quit the premises, she was mine before you ever saw her."

This made him furious, and he called me a low-down liar, and swore that Belette was his, and that I should never touch a hair of her head.

"Do you ever look at yourself in the glass, my poor friend?" said I. "She is meat for your masters, in other words for me, so go back where you came from and dig turnips."

"Listen to me, Breugnon," said he. "She loves me best." —I shook my head. "Will you leave it to her?" he persisted, "and promise to get out if she takes me?"

"Agreed!" said I, and held out my hand.

It is one thing to tell a girl to choose, but it is quite another to make her do it; there is much more fun for her in keeping two suitors on the string; so she merely laughed in our faces, and went off, when we told her of our bargain. We were really fond of one another, but now, there was nothing else for it, we had to fight. Back we went to the shop, and pulled our coats off.

"Hold on a second," said Pinon, and gave me a great kiss on both cheeks. Then we went at it in earnest, for when it comes to real fighting, friendship has to go to the wall, and in five minutes Pinon had nearly knocked my head off, while I battered at his stomach, till the blood literally poured off both of us. How it would have ended, no one knows, for by this time we were as savage as a couple of bulldogs; but my Master Lagneau and some of the neighbors heard the row and rushed in. A hard time they had to pull us apart, and at last Lagneau had even to take his horsewhip to us, but they finally made us let go, and a sight we were to behold when it was over! At this crisis the third party made his appearance; he was a miller named Jean Mifflard, short and red in the face, with little eyes like a wild boar's, and fat puffy cheeks. He laughed at the pair of us; and told us we were fools to knock each other about for a little hussy like that, who was only amusing herself at our expense, just for the fun of trailing a pack of lovers at her heels.

"I will tell you what," said he: "she is only making game of you; so now, just shake hands and go off somewhere together, that will turn the laugh on her, and when she finds that you are gone out of her reach, she will be forced to choose, one way or the other, and let the best man win! Now then! get out with you! and the sooner the better. You may rely on me while you are gone, to keep an eye on the lady, and if anything new turns up, you shall know it. Come on and have a drink, and forget all about it!"

We did drink, I can tell you, — my word, but we were thirsty! — and that very night we started off together for nowhere in particular; proud enough of ourselves, God knows why! and with hearts full of gratitude towards our friend the miller, who laughed when he took leave of us till his little eyes almost disappeared under his fat eyelids.

The next morning, though we did not like to admit it, we felt a little less cocky — and we sat and thought of this precious plan of attacking a place by running away from it, and as the sun rose higher in the heavens, our respect for ourselves sank lower, till by nightfall we were watching each other like two cats, though we still kept up a show of indifference. In the back of our minds was the notion of stealing off alone to the village, but neither of us dared to take his eye off the other for a second. Each tried all sorts of unsuccessful dodges to get rid of the other man, but finally we lay down on our straw mattresses, pretending to fall asleep and snore loudly, though love and fleas chased rest from our eyelids.

At last Pinon could bear it no longer, and jumped up, declaring that he was going back. "All right then," said I, "I'm with you!"

It took us a whole day to walk home; but we got there about sunset, and hid in the woods till dark, as we were not particularly anxious for any one to see us, — it would have been rather awkward, and then we wanted to surprise Belette; — we pictured her in tears, reproaching herself, sighing for her lost lover; — which one? — but you can guess what answer each of us gave to that question.

Our hearts beat fast as we stole down to the end of her garden; the moonlight shone full on the cottage, and what do you think I saw hanging on an apple-tree just outside of her open window? Not an apple, no, it was a hat belonging to Giffard, the miller!

There is no need to dwell on what followed, though of course every one but ourselves would have thought it killingly funny. I stayed where I was, but Quiriace made one jump, swung himself up the tree, ran along the branch, and leaped in at the window.

In a moment the air was rent with screams, curses, yells, and vituperations, noise of breaking furniture, smashed china and glass, groans, blows, shrieks, and growls, as if a cage full of wild beasts were fighting. As you may imagine, the row soon woke up the entire neighborhood; I did not wait to see the end of it, but made off as fast as I could, half laughing, — for it was funny when you came to think of it, — but with the tears running down my cheeks all the same.

"You are well out of that, Colas my boy," said I to myself, but in my heart I was not so sure of it. I tried to laugh at all the row-de-dow, and mimic the girl, Quiriace, and the miller. "But oh! Belette," cried I, "this will break my heart!"

I didn't really know if I was glad or sorry, but on the whole I came near to regretting my escape; for if I had married her, and she had betrayed me? At least she would have been mine, and love is well worth any price you must pay for it.

For at least a month I was drawn to and fro between rage and relief; while the whole village split its sides laughing at me, and sometimes, when the thought of Belette came over me I could have dashed my head against the wall. Fortunately such feelings do not last; we are not meant to die for love, but to live by it; and then you do not often find a hero of romance in Burgundy; life is too sweet to us for that; and since our permission was not asked before we were born, we feel that we may as well make the best of it now that we are here. We need the world, or the world needs us, I was never quite sure which; but at all events we always hold on till the last gasp, draining every drop of the cup, and when it is empty, we can fill it up again from our bounteous hillsides. No native of Burgundy is in a hurry to die; but when it comes to suffering, we can bear it as well as the best.

Well, for as much as six months, I was deucedly unhappy; but time flows along, and sweeps our sorrows away with it. Now that it is all over, I can find consolation, but oh, my Belette! if only I had not missed you!—and that pig-faced miller, with his flour bags! to think that all these years she has belonged to him!—thirty years ago he married her!

They tell me that he began to neglect her almost from the first day, (he was just the kind of animal that bolts his food, and so gets no flavor out of it); and they say too that he would not have married her at all, if Pinon had not caught him that night, and forced him, so to speak, into a wedding ring, which was too tight for him and her too; for when things were not to his liking, he naturally took it out of his wife. So there was an end of one, two and three, Pinon, Belette, and poor old Breugnon, who has been trying, ever since, to make a joke of it. ... I could scarcely believe my eyes when at a turn in the path, I saw her house not twenty yards away; was it possible that I had been walking for hours among those old memories? There was the red roof, and the white walls of the cottage, half covered with the rich foliage of a grapevine, its thick stem winding upwards like a serpent. The door stood open; before it in the shade of a walnut tree was a stone trough running over with clear water. A woman was stooping over it and my knees gave way under me when I saw her again after all these years. My first impulse was to run, but she had seen me, and as she dipped her pail in the trough she still kept her eyes on me, and I felt that she knew who I was, though she was far too proud to show it. The next moment the bucket slipped from her fingers as she straightened herself up, and then she called out, "Better late than never!"

"That sounds as if you had been waiting for me!"

"What an idea! I don't believe that I have given you one thought in twenty years."

"Nor I either," said I, "but all the same, it does me good to see you."

"And me too," she answered, crossing her wet arms, and looking at me as I stood there in my shirt-sleeves. Our eyes met and yet we could not seem to look each other in the face; between us the water filled and ran over the rim of the bucket, and at last she spoke again, "Come in and sit down a minute."

"I must be getting on, thank you," I said, "as I am rather in a hurry."

"Slow to come, and quick to go," said she. "I don't see why you came at all, then?"

"I was only taking a stroll about here," said I calmly.

"Money and time must be cheap where you come from."

"Oh! when I get an idea in my head I never count the cost."

"The same old looney still I see!" said she, laughing, and "Once a fool, always a fool!" was my answer. We walked slowly in, and she closed the yard gate behind us, shutting us in alone, among the hens which clucked about our feet. She crossed over and shut,—or maybe opened,—the big doors of the barn, and spoke a word to the watch-dog, but I saw that it was to cover her embarrassment, and that all the men were off in the fields. I talked as fast as I could, about farming, chicken raising, pigeons, ducks, pigs, and all the creatures that ever came out of the ark; but all at once she stopped me.

"Breugnon!" My breath came short as I looked at her. "Breugnon," she said again, and then, "Kiss me!" My lips were on hers, before the words were well off them, and though at our age there is not much to be got out of kissing, it is always a pleasure, and it fairly brought the tears to my eyes to feel her soft wrinkled cheeks against mine.

"Old silly!" said I to myself; "what is there to cry for?"

"You are as bristly as a hedgehog!" she said, laughing.

"Excuse me! I would have given myself an extra shave this morning if I had known the pleasure that was in store for me, but it is a fact that my beard was softer thirty years ago when I would, and you wouldn't, you little minx of a shepherdess!"

"Do you ever think now of those old times?"

"No, I have forgotten all about them." We laughed, but neither could look at the other.

"You are something like me," she said. "As proud as a peacock, as stubborn as a mule, and what is more, I can see you are the kind that will never grow old. You were no beauty in your best days, my friend, and when a man has nothing, you can't take it away from him; perhaps your nose may be rather thicker, and you have plenty of wrinkles, but on the whole you are not much the worse for wear. I always say that the main thing is to keep the hair on one's head, and yours is not white yet, and as thick as ever."

"Numskull keeps the thatch full," said I.

"You men are so aggravating, you never let anything bother you, but we poor creatures grow old, because we have all the weight thrown on our shoulders; see what a wreck I am! once I was like a fresh peach to look at, and to touch too, if you remember? Such hair as I had! such skin, such a figure, and where has it all gone now? Own up now, you would not have known me if you had met me in the street?"

"I would have known you anywhere out of all the women in the world, with my eyes shut."

"Perhaps so, but if they were open? I have lost teeth, my cheeks have fallen in, I have red eyes, and a sharp nose; while as for my throat and all the rest of it, I am nothing but an old meal sack, and that's the truth!"

"In my eyes you are always young."

"You must be blind, then."

"No, Belette, my sight at least is as keen as ever. Do you remember? You were called that because you were like a little weasel, and here you are, run to earth, after all your doublings and turnings, and you still have your little sharp nose, and bright eyes like your namesake, shining up at me out of your burrow."

"It's safe enough now, at any rate, for the old fox to come near me. Well, love has not made you any thinner."

"Why should it?" said I, laughing. "The creature has to be fed!"

"Perhaps it would do as well to give him something to drink," said she, so we went into the farmhouse, and sat down at the table. The Lord knows what it was that she placed before me! I was too much taken up with other things to notice, but all the time I plied a good knife and fork as usual, while she sat opposite with her elbows on the table, and when our eyes met, she gave me a smile.

"Are you feeling a little better?"

"Stomach empty, heart heavy, belly full, heart light! that's what the old song tells us," said I. She was silent, but her big clever mouth twitched at the corners, and I kept on talking of the first thing that came into my head, while we looked at one another, and thought of all that had passed between us.

"Breugnon," said she, at last, "I can tell you, now that it does not matter, it was you I was in love with."

"I knew it all the time," said I calmly.

"And if you knew so much, why did you say nothing about it?"

"Because, of course, you would have been just perverse enough to contradict me."

"What difference would that have made, if you had been sure of the contrary? You kiss people's lips, not the words that come out of them!"

"Something more than words used to come out of your lips, on occasion. — Do you remember that night we caught you with the miller?"

"It was all your fault," she said, "or mine, if you like to say so, but, Colas, you that have so much penetration, did you know one thing? I took him out of pure spite, because you went off that time with Pinon? I had been angry with you for a long time, ever since that evening, — I don't know if you recollect it, — when you despised me."

"I? Never in the world!"

"Yes, you, surely you remember one evening when I fell asleep in the garden, and you came and picked me up, but dropped me like a hot potato?" — "Belette," said I earnestly, "let me tell you all about it."

"Don't trouble yourself," said she, "but how if it were to do over again?"

"I think that I should do just the same."

"What a mutton-head it is!" cried she. "But on my soul! I believe that is the reason why I loved you,—still I thought I would have some fun with you, after that; you deserved to suffer a little, and who could have thought that you would be fool enough to go away from the hook, instead of swallowing it?"

"Much obliged!" said I; "but hooks have sharp points to them."

She laughed, and looked at me in the old way under her lashes. "Well, when I heard of your fight with that other blockhead, whose name I have forgotten, (I was down by the river washing my clothes, when I heard some one say that he was tearing you to pieces), I dropped the basket and let everything float away in the water, and ran off just as I was in my bare feet, trampling on everybody in my way. I was all out of breath, but I wanted to call out that I loved you, that I could not bear to have that great brute bite you to pieces, that I wanted a whole husband not the remains of one;—but when I got there the fight was over, and my fine gentlemen were guzzling in the tavern, on the best of terms. Then the lamb and the wolf ran away together, leaving me in such a fury! It seems ridiculous now when I look at you, but at that moment I should have liked to tear the skin off your back; and since I could not get at you to punish you, I punished myself. In my rage I took up with the first man who came along;—the miller. Revenge is sweet, but I swear that it was you that I thought of all the time when—"

"I know what you mean," said I.

"Well," she continued, "I kept thinking that I hoped Breugnon's ears would burn when he heard it, that it served him right, that I wished that he would come back now; and you did come back, rather sooner than I intended and,—you know what happened, so there I was, tied for life to my donkey, and here we are both of us."

After a pause I said, "I hope at least that you get on pretty well with him?"

"About as well as he does with me," she answered, with a shrug of her shoulders.

I could not help saying, "Your home must be Paradise."

"You've hit the mark," said she, laughing.

After that we changed the conversation, and talked of everything on earth; farms, cattle, and children, but try as we would, we could not keep away from the old subject. I thought perhaps that it would interest her to hear all about me and mine; but I soon found that she was too much of a woman not to have known long ago all that I could tell her; so we went on from one thing to another, up and down, in and out, just for the sake of talking. We were both great at puns, and jokes of that kind; and it would have taken your breath away to hear the cross fire of wit between us; and quick! — we fairly snatched the words out of each other's mouths, and laughed till the tears ran down our cheeks.

All at once six strokes sounded from the clock in the corner. "Six already!" said I; "it is time that I was going."

"Plenty of time," said she.

"I suppose your husband will be here in a few moments," said I, "and to tell the truth, I am not so very anxious to meet him."

"That's just the way I feel," she answered.

I looked out of the kitchen window at the meadows, all golden now with the rays of the setting sun which shone between the long grass blades. Down by the stream two cows were standing in the water, and a little bird hopped about on the shining pebbles. A black horse, with a star on his forehead, and a dapple gray were standing there; the black with his head resting on the back of the other. The fresh scent of hay and lilacs blew through the open door; the room was dark and the least bit musty; and I could just sniff the good cherry brandy from the mug before me. "You have a nice place of it here," I could not help saying.

"How much nicer if you had been in it all this time!" she said, putting her hand over mine as it lay on the table. It made me almost sorry that I had come, for of course I did not want her to be unhappy.

"Belette," said I, "perhaps on the whole things are better as they are; we get along well enough like this for an hour or two, but if we had had to spend our lives together, you know that there would have been trouble. Surely you must have heard that I have turned out rather badly: a dreamer, a talker, always dawdling about, backbiting and quarreling, and sticking my nose into other folk's business. I am an idler too, and drink more than is good for me; all this would have made you unhappy, and then you would have taken up with some one else; it makes my hair stand on end only to think of it! So you see all is really for the best."

She heard me to the end, and then said seriously: "Yes, I know you are a perfect good-for-nothing, (she did not believe a word of it); probably you would have beaten me, and perhaps I should have taken a lover, but if that was our destiny, it might as well have come to us through each other." I nodded my head. "You don't seem to be of my mind?"

"I am, of course," said I, "but, you see that kind of happiness was not for us; so now, Belette, there is no use in self-reproaches, or regrets either. It would have been all the same by this time, whatever we had done; we are at the end of our string now, you know, and love or no love, it is all past like a tale that is told."

"Liar!" said she, and I felt that she spoke the truth, even as I looked at her.

I kissed her once more, and left her; she leaned against the door-post looking after me, under the great spreading branches of the walnut-tree, but I did not turn my head till I got round the corner, where I was sure that I could not see her; then I stopped to take breath a minute, and enjoy the scent of the honeysuckle. Down in the meadows I could see the white oxen still grazing as I left the path and took a short cut up the hillside and through the vines, until I got into the wood, where I turned aside for a moment. This was not the shortest way to continue my journey, but, there I stood for as much as half an hour, leaning against the trunk of a big oak tree, with my eyes fixed on vacancy, thinking, thinking. I could see the last red reflections of the western sky die out on the fresh vine leaves, which shone as if varnished, and hear the first faint note of a nightingale singing. I remembered an evening when my love and I were climbing side by side, up the steep vineyard, laughing and talking as we went, vigorous as the young life around us; but in the midst of our mirth, suddenly we fell silent, my hand closed on hers and there we stood motionless. Was it the sound of the Angelus, the evening breeze sighing about us, or the soft moonlight? From the shadowy vine leaves all at once arose the voice of a nightingale singing to keep himself awake, so that the treacherous tendrils might not twine about his poor little feet, and hold him prisoner, singing his eternal love-song; and I held Belette's hand, saying: "The tendrils are around us, and like them we cling to each other."

Then we went back down the hill again, still hand in hand, till we reached her cottage.

That was the last time that our fingers clung thus together, but the nightingale's note still sounds, the vine puts forth its branches, and love still twists young hearts in its supple tendrils. Night came on, as I stood there, gazing up at the silvered treetops. I could not tear myself away from that magic shadow which dimmed my homeward path, and even destroyed the wish to find it. Three times I tried, but found myself back where I started, so I gave it up, and took a lodging for that night at the sign of the Moonbeam. It was not a very good inn to sleep in: I lay there turning over the pages of my life, thinking of what I had done and left undone, and of the dreams from which I had awakened. In such dark hours what sadness rises from the depths of our hearts, what vanished hopes!—How far off seem the bright visions of early boyhood, and how poor and bare the reality looks. I thought of all my expectations, and the small results of my labors; of my wife, who certainly cannot be called either good-natured or good-looking, of my sons who hardly seem to belong to me, with whom I have nothing in common:— of the faithlessness and folly of those around us, of our poor France torn by civil wars and religious persecutions; of my works of art scattered, life itself a handful of ashes, soon to be blown away by the breath of the Destroyer.—I put my face close up against the oak-tree, and lay there weeping quietly all among the big roots which cradled me like a father's arms; and I felt that he listened, and consoled me, for when, many hours later, I awoke, I found myself snoring with my nose in a tuft of moss, with nothing remaining of my troubles but a sore feeling in my heart, and a slight cramp in the calf of my leg.

The sun was just rising, and the tree above me was so full of birds that it dripped with their singing like a ripe bunch of grapes. The robin, the linnet, and my special favorite, the thrush, sang as if to bursting. — I like Master Thrush because he does not care for any weather, is the first to begin singing, and the last to stop, and like me, is always in a good humor. — They had all passed safely through the dangers of the night, which darkens their little lives every twenty-four hours, but as soon as the curtain begins to rise, and the first ray of dawn puts fresh color into life — Twee-ee, twee, twee, twee, tweet! with what sweet cries and transports of joy they greet the new day. In the glory of the morning all is forgotten, the dark night, the cold and the terrors. If only the birds could teach us the secret of their unalterable faith, through which they are born afresh with every dawning day!

All this merry whistling cheered me up wonderfully, and lying there on my back, I began to whistle too, the same tune; pretty soon from the wood where he was hiding came the cry of the cuckoo. I could lie still no longer, and jumped gaily to my feet; a hare near by followed my example, seeming to laugh at me as he passed; (you know he once split his lip open by too much laughter). Then at last I started off towards home, singing at the top of my lungs. All is good, the sky, the wood. Oh! my friends the world is round, if you can't swim, you will be drowned. Throw open all the windows of your five senses, and let the great earth in. What is the use of sulking because everything does not come your way? The more you sulk, the less you get. I do not suppose that the Duke, the King, or even God Himself, has all the desire of his heart; ought I to groan and struggle, because I cannot exceed the limits set for me? Should I even be better off if I could get outside of them? No, no, I have nothing to complain of in this world, and I mean to stay here as long as I possibly can. Suppose that I had never been born? I really cannot bear to think of a world without Breugnon, or what is perhaps even worse, Breugnon without the world! A plague on all such nonsense! things are well enough as they are, and you may be sure that I shall hold tight to all that belongs to me.

When I got back to Clamecy, I was a whole day behind time, and you may guess what sort of a welcome I had, and also how little I minded. I just shut myself up in the garret, and put it all down on paper, as you see. There was no one there to listen, so if the fancy took me I could speak out loud, going over in retrospect all that happened, both pleasures and pains, and the pleasure that we get out of pain, for —

> *"That which breaks the heart to bear,*
> *Is sometimes sweet to tell and hear."*

VI
Birds of Passage
or
The Serenade at Asnois

WE heard yesterday morning that Clamecy was to entertain two distinguished guests, the Demoiselle de Termes and the Comte de Maillebois; they were on their way to the Château of Asnois, where they were to stay for a month or so. The Town Council, according to usage, voted to send a delegation to our noble visitors in the name of the city, in order to offer them our congratulations on their safe arrival (as if it were a miracle to come from Paris to Nevers in a warm easy carriage without upsetting or losing your way!) It being also the custom to make a little present, the Council decided to add some cakes with icing, made in Clamecy, of which we are not a little proud. My son-in-law, Florimond Ravisé, is our principal pastry cook, so he proposed to send three dozen, which was opposed by the Council, who thought two dozen would be plenty; however, Florimond being an alderman, his views prevailed, and the cakes were baked at the expense of the town. Some one suggested that noble ears ought to be tickled at the same time as the palate; so in order that the exalted strangers should listen to a serenade while they were enjoying our cakes, and have all their senses charmed at once, we chose also four of our best musicians, two violas, two hautboys, a tambourine, and a flageolet player—myself. In point of fact I was not invited, but I never miss a chance to see a new face if I can help it, and I was particularly anxious to behold these Court birds of paradise with their shining plumage, and all their airs and graces; besides, I adore any novelty, wherever it comes from,—like a true son of Pandora. If I had my way I would soon take the lid off all the boxes, or souls, within my reach, black or white, thick or thin, high or low; I like to poke my nose into affairs that are none of my business, to find out secrets of the heart, and generally know all that goes on; in a word, I am devoured by curiosity, but as there is no reason, as far as I can see, why one should not add profit to pleasure, I took with me two fine carved panels, which the Seigneur of Asnois had ordered and which were easily stowed away on one of the carts provided by the town to carry the delegation, the musical instruments, and the iced cakes. My little Glodie went too, because she was Florimond's daughter, and it cost nothing; and another alderman took his little boy, if I remember rightly. Finally the apothecary stuck in a lot of sweetmeats, spirits, and cordials of his own manufacture; also of course at the expense of the city. Florimond was indignant, and protested with some reason; he said if every butcher, baker, and candlestick maker were to do the same, the town would be ruined; but there was no use in talking, as the other man was equally a member of the Council with himself, and as we all know, great men make laws and the rest obey them.

Our two carts were soon loaded with the Mayor, the panels, the presents, the children, four musicians, and four Councilors. I went on foot, however, for I am not yet so feeble as to be dragged about in a cart, like a calf on its way to the butcher. The weather was not quite to my liking, for the air was close and sultry, with a sun hot enough to roast you beating down on our heads, and clouds of dust and flies about us; we none of us minded, however, as we were out on a spree; Florimond was peevish, but then he is always bothering, like a girl, about his complexion.

Our worthy citizens sat up very stiff and proper as long as we could see St. Martin's tower, but when we got well outside the town, all formality dropped off, and left us, as you may say, in our shirt-sleeves. We cracked a few rather doubtful jokes, for that is the way we generally begin, and then there was singing; his honor the Mayor leading off, while I accompanied him on the flageolet, and the rest joined in the chorus. In the midst of all the voices and instruments I could hear my little Glodie's shrill sweet pipe like a sparrow.

We did not get on very fast, because the nags would stop on top of every hill to get their breath, and then when we came to Boychault, our scrivener, Pierre Delavau, begged us to go out of our way a little, and we could not very well say no, for he was the only Alderman who had so far asked no favors, so we had to stop to let him draw up a will for one of his clients, which was rather a long business; but no one really objected except Florimond, who this time had the apothecary on his side. All the same Master Delavau drew out the document at his leisure, and the others had to put up with it as best they could.

We got to the château at last;—you always do, in the end, and there were the fine Court birds just leaving the table, so the dessert we brought came in at the right moment. Down they sat and began all over again; you never saw such birds for eating; and now we made a brilliant entrance, for our delegation had halted outside the gates to put on their carefully folded robes, which they had been sitting on all the way to keep them from fading. The Mayor's was of bright green silk, and the others woolen of a light yellow, so that they looked like a cucumber and four pumpkins as we marched into the courtyard to the sound of our instruments. Every window in the castle was filled with heads at our approach, and our courtly guests deigned to show themselves in the doorway, all curled and beribboned, as the green and yellow Mayor and Council mounted the great staircase. We smaller fry, musicians and others, stayed behind in the yard, so that I could not hear very clearly the fine Latin discourse delivered by our notary; which mattered the less, as I do believe Master Pierre himself was the only one who did hear it. But the one thing I would not have missed for a kingdom was the sight of my darling Glodie stepping carefully upward with the basket piled high with cakes clasped tight in her little arms. She was like pictures of the Presentation. Sweetheart! I longed to hug her! Music is not the only thing which charms all heart; childhood has a spell even stronger and more universal, which causes the proudest to forget for the moment rank and dignity. Mademoiselle de Termes could not help smiling at Glodie, then she took her up on her knees and kissed her, and finally broke one of the famous cakes in two, ate half herself, and as she said laughing, "Open your little beak, birdie," stuck the other half into the child's rosy mouth. "Hurrah for the Flower of Nevers!" I shouted, and then played a gay little phrase on my flute, which sounded like the note of a swallow. This made every one laugh, and as they all looked to see who was playing Glodie clapped her hands and said, "That is my Grandad." And so Monsieur d'Asnois made a sign to me to come up, and said to those about him, "You really ought to see Breugnon, he is just the least bit cracked." (I am no more cracked than he is, but I went up as I was bid, with a fine bow to the company.)

All the time that I was bowing and scraping to right and left, I had my eye on the noble lady, hung like a slender bell-clapper in the midst of her spreading draperies; and I could not help wondering how she would look if divested of her voluminous garments, — (a bold idea for a man like me, but only an idea, of course, or you will wonder how I dared to think of such a thing), for she was tall and thin, rather dark-skinned under a thick coating of powder; her hair fell in ringlets over her great brown eyes shining like carbuncles; she had full red lips and a small pointed nose like a ferret; you should have seen the condescending air with which she said to me, "This charming little girl is your grandchild, they tell me."

"Madam," said I, in my best manner, "I must refer you to my son-in-law, here present, for an answer to that question; but you may be sure that as she is not made of money we do not quarrel over her, — the poor, you know, find their wealth in their children."

She was so kind as to smile at my pleasantry, and my Lord of Asnois burst out laughing. Florimond laughed too, but not so heartily, and I remained as grave as a judge. Then his Lordship and the lady deigned to enter into conversation with me about my trade, and what I made by it, for they took it for granted that I was a minstrel. I told them I made little or nothing, which was true enough, but as they had not asked me I did not say what I did for my living, but let them go on talking while

I laughed in my sleeve at the airs they gave themselves, the haughty familiarity with which these fine gentlemen of rank and wealth treat us poor devils. They speak to a poor man as if he were a child, or half-witted. God has so ordered it that only the unworthy are at the bottom of the ladder, — (that is what they think, if they would only admit it), and therefore praise be to the Lord! who has exalted the seats of the mighty!

The Lord of Maillebois spoke to his companion as if I were not within hearing. "Madame," said he, "we may as well fill up our time and have a little talk with this fellow; he seems rather stupid, but as he goes about from one tavern to another, playing on his flageolet, he probably knows what people hereabouts are thinking."

"Hush!"

"If indeed they can be said to think at all."

So they said to me:

"Well, my man, tell us what ideas prevail in the province?"

"Ideas?" said I, as if I had never heard the word before, looking slyly at our good Lord of Asnois, who laughed to himself under his big bushy beard, but let me go on.

"Ideas do not seem to grow plentifully in this part of the country," said Maillebois with his heavy playfulness, "but I mean I want to know what the people are thinking, — are they loyal to Church and King?"

"God is great, and so is His Majesty; we are devoted to both of them."

"And how about the Princes?"

"They too are great gentlemen." — "Do you mean that you are on their side?" — "Yes, indeed, my Lord, we are close beside them."

"In that case you must be against Concini?" — "By no means, your Lordship, we are for him also."

"But, man, you don't seem to understand that they are enemies."

"That may be — but we want both of them to succeed."

"How absurd! You have to be on one side or the other, don't you know that? Stupid!"

"Must I really, my Lord? Can't I get out of it? Well, if I must, I must, only let me think it over; a man can't make up his mind like that all in a minute!"

"Why, what in the world are you waiting for?" — "Only to know which will come out on top!" — "You ought to be ashamed of yourself, you rascal! Do you mean that you have not sense enough to know light from darkness, or the King from his enemies?"

I explained with an air of perfect simplicity that I was not so blinded but that I could tell day from night, but that when it came to the King or the Princes, if I was forced to choose between them, I could not tell which party drank most, or did the greatest harm to the country. "Far be it from me," said I, "to speak evil of dignities. I wish them all good health and prosperity. To you too, your noble Lordship! They have fine appetites and I am something of a hearty eater myself, but to make a clean breast of it, if they must eat, I had rather it should be at some one's else expense!" — "Do you respect nothing, fellow?" — "I respect and love my own belongings." — "Don't you know that it is your duty to make sacrifices for the King, your master?"

I told him respectfully that I should be only too glad to do so if there was no way of getting out of it, but I asked him to explain to me how it happened that there were the people of France, who loved their fields and their vineyards, and there also was the King who wanted only to devour them; — I said I knew well enough that every one had his place in the world, and some were made to eat and some to be eaten; politics I had heard was the art of filling your own stomach, and that was an art reserved for the noble, and the land for the peasant. But what was a poor man to do, since he was not allowed to have an opinion? And besides, as we are all as ignorant as our father Adam, (they say that he was his Lordship's father also, but I could not well believe it, maybe he was only a cousin) — our business is to plow and enrich the soil, to sow and reap, to plant vines and gather grapes, make wine and bread, work in wood and stone, in cloth and leather; lay out canals and highways, erect great cathedrals and cities adorned with gardens, and embellish with carving and statues; catch sound and imprison it in the flanks of a fiddle, make ourselves masters, in short, of France, the earth and the air above us; — all to add to the pleasure of our lords. How could the people be expected to go any farther and try to grasp the high designs of kings, the quarrels of princes, with all their politics and metaphysics? No, the stick is made for beasts of burden, but which cudgel is the softest and who is to shake it over our backs, is a question too hard for us to decide; if we had the stick in our own hands for a little while it might be easier, but in the meantime there is nothing for it but patience, and to bear the blows as long as we are the anvil; some day our turn will come at the hammer! While I was talking, the Seigneur of Maillebois stood looking at me, in two minds whether to laugh or be angry; fortunately one of his equerries had seen me one day when I was with the late Duke, and he explained who I was, that I was no minstrel, but a fine sculptor and worker in wood, known far and wide for my talk, and somewhat of a free thinker.

The noble Lord did not seem much impressed by this information, but he showed a faint interest in my insignificant personality when his host told him that my work had been admired by princes of his acquaintance, and he soon fell into ecstasies when they showed him the fountain I had made in the courtyard. It is a girl with her skirts tucked up, holding two ducks in her apron with their wings extended; the water trickles out of their beaks; — a pretty conceit as I think it. He saw also my carved furniture and panels in the castle, which Asnois displayed with as much pride as if he had been their creator instead of being merely the man who paid for them. Maillebois expressed himself as astonished that I should bury my talent so far from Paris, and he also wondered that I should confine myself to work which showed chiefly observation and fidelity to nature; no grandeur or symbolism, nothing allegorical, both things which the critic considers essential to great sculpture. (A lord, you know, admires nothing that is not lordly.)

To which I replied with due respect, as became a country booby, that I knew my place, and was always careful to keep in it; that it would be presumption for a poor man like me, without knowledge or education, to attempt anything vast or sublime, and that he ought to be content with a modest place on the lowest step of Mount Parnassus, aiming only at such things as may be useful in everyday life. Utility in art should be his motto.

"Utility in art!" exclaimed his Lordship; "that is a contradiction in terms, true beauty is only found in what is useless."

"A lofty sentiment," said I, bowing, "and profoundly true; you see it everywhere, in art as well as in life; a diamond is beautiful, and so is a king, a prince, a great noble, or a flower."

On this he turned away, much pleased with so much proper feeling; but Asnois pinched me, and whispered in my ear, "Shut up, you old humbug! I don't mind if you do make a fool of this fop from Paris, but don't try anything of that sort on me, or it will be the worse for you!"

"Oh! your Lordship, how could you think me capable of such a thing? As if I would be so ungrateful to my protector, my benefactor! and not only ungrateful but foolish. Breugnon is not that kind of a fool, he knows enough to take good care of his own skin, and your Lordship is not only stronger, — that is as it should be, — but ever so much cleverer than I am. What chance should I have against an old fox like the Lord of Asnois, if I may venture to say so? You who get the better of young and old, gentle and simple."

Nothing is so agreeable as to be praised for talents which we do not possess; so he fairly beamed as he answered, "Your tongue is long enough in all conscience, but now I should like to know what brought you here today? For I'll be bound you were after something."

"There now, what was I saying just this minute? You see through a man as if he were a pane of glass; like God Almighty, the heart has no secrets from your Lordship." Then of course I unpacked my two panels, and also something else I had brought, namely an Italian piece picked up at Mantua, representing Fortune on her wheel, which, through a mistake I am at a loss to account for, I claimed as my own. It did not excite much admiration. Then I showed a medallion of a girl's head, done by me, as the product of an Italian chisel, and it received a perfect ovation! you never heard such ohs! and ahs! The Lord of Maillebois was particularly enthusiastic; he said he could detect in this admirable work the influence of a land twice blessed by Heaven, — by Jupiter and by Jesus Christ; and the Lord of Asnois ended by giving me thirty-six ducats for it, — but I only got three for the Fortune!

As we were coming home that evening I told my friends a little anecdote which I thought would amuse them. The Duke of Bellegarde came some years ago to Clamecy to shoot at the popinjay, but as he was short-sighted, I was hidden behind the target, and instructed to throw down the wooden bird as soon as he fired, and in its place to substitute as quickly as possible a bird with a hole through the middle. We all laughed at this story, and then each in his turn had some such thing to tell of our noble masters. If they could only hear some of the jokes we have at their expense, they would not be quite so bored perhaps in the midst of their royal grandeur. Nothing was said, you may be sure, about the medallion till we were safe at home, and the door shut, and then Florimond was much vexed with me because I had sold the Italian piece at such a low price as my own, seeing that they had been willing to pay anything I asked for the other; but as I said, I liked to laugh at people but not to skin them; that naturally made him crosser than ever, and he wanted to know what fun I could find in cheating myself? And if there was any sport in making a mock of people unless there was something to be gained by it?

"Florimond," said my daughter Martine gravely, "we were all like that at home, always jolly and ready for a good story. You ought not to complain of that sort of disposition, for it is much to your advantage, and it is lucky for you that the idea that I could deceive you at any moment is so amusing to me that I don't care to do it. Now don't put on that gloomy air; you know the proverb, 'No need to cry out before you are hurt.'"

VII
The Plague

WE have recently had reason to feel the full truth of the old saying: "Evil comes on a swift horse, but is slow of foot to leave us." This time we had hardly any warning, for on Monday of last week we heard of the first case of the plague at St. Fargeau, and the evil seed sprang up so rapidly that by the end of the week there were ten more cases and yesterday it broke out here in our neighborhood at Coulanges-la-Vineuse. You can imagine what a clatter there was in our duck-pond, and how the boldest took to their heels! Most of the women and children were packed off to Montenoison to be out of danger; leaving an unwonted calm behind them, at least in my household; it's an ill wind that blows no one good!

Florimond went in charge of the female detachment, on the pretext that he could not leave Martine, as she was near her confinement, but he was kept in countenance by many another gentleman, who, when his carriage was at the door, thought it was a good time to go and see how the crops were getting on at a distance. We who stayed behind put a good face on it, and had no end of fun out of the people who were frightened, and their precautions. The Provost stationed guards at the town gates, and on the road to Auxerre, with strict orders to turn back any tramps or beggars who might attempt to enter, and even the well-to-do, whose purses at least were perfectly healthy, had to be examined by our three physicians, Messrs. Etienne Loyseau, Martin Frotier, and Philibert des Veaux, all fortified against the plague by means of masks, spectacles, and long false noses filled with unguents. Everybody laughed so much at them that Frotier could bear it no longer, and tore off his nose, declaring that he for his part had no faith in such nonsense; all the same, poor old chap, he died of it, but so did Loyseau also, who kept his nose on, and shared a bed with him. The only survivor of the three was des Veaux, who was better advised than his colleagues, and abandoned his post instead of his precautions. But I have got ahead of my story and must go back and begin again at the beginning. We all whistled loudly to keep our courage up, declaring that our tanneries would keep off the pestilence, as it is well known that there is nothing so healthy as the smell of leather. The last visitation we had had of the plague was about the year 1580 (I remember it well, for I was nearly fourteen years old); she poked her nose then over our threshold, but came no farther, to the astonishment of all our neighbors, particularly those of Châtel-Censoir, who were so disgusted with their patron, St. Potentian, who had not taken good care of them, that they turned him out, and tried seven others in succession, until in despair they fell back on a female of the same name, St. Potentiana. We told this, and lots of other old stories, with shouts of laughter; and to show that we were above such silly superstitions, and had no faith in the Provost's regulations either, we went boldly down to the Chastelot gate and talked across the moat with all the vagrants assembled there. Some of us even slipped out between the angels who stood guard before our paradise, — (they did not take themselves seriously either), and shared a bottle with some of these outcasts in a nearby tavern. Need I say that I was one of the number? for naturally I could not bear the thought that the others should go swaggering, drinking and talking, and I not of the party. I met a friend out there, a farmer from Mailly-le-Château, and we had a drink together. He was a jolly old bird with a round red face fairly shining with health and good cheer, and he was even more boastful about the plague than I was, pooh-poohing the whole thing and declaring that it was all an invention of the doctors and that people died of fear, and not of the pestilence; said he, "I'll tell you the best remedy I know for it, and I won't charge you anything either!"

> *"Be sure and warm your feet;*
> *Be careful what you eat;*
> *Be shy of woman's charm,*
> *And you are safe from harm."*

We sat there with our heads together for an hour or more; he had a trick of poking you in the ribs, or slapping you on the back or the leg, which I did not notice much at the time, but you may believe I thought of it afterwards, when the next morning one of my apprentices told me that old farmer Grattepain was dead! It made the cold shivers go down my back, and in my heart I gave myself up for lost, but I went back to the shop and fussed about a little, though I was hardly conscious of what I was about, and kept saying to myself, "You have done for yourself now, you old idiot." Still, in our part of the world we don't waste time over what we ought to have done the day before yesterday, we just take hold and do what we can at the present moment; so I resolved to keep the enemy at bay as long as I was able, telling myself that I still had a good fighting chance. The idea of consulting a doctor occurred to me (going to St. Cosmo's shop, as we call it), but in spite of the trouble I was in, I had enough self-control not to do it, for, as I said to myself, doctors really know no more than we do, they will only take my fee, and send me to the pest-house, and there I shall catch the plague and no mistake; no, so long as I have my wits about me, I will ask help of no man; dying is, after all, a lonely business, and as the saying goes, "In spite of every drug and leech, we live until Death's door we reach."

All this time, in spite of my bravado, I began to have queer feelings in my stomach, in my head, and all over my body; I cannot get over it when I think of the delicious dish of mutton and beans, dressed with wine sauce, which I actually refused at dinner time. I could not swallow a mouthful; thought I, "This is final; if my appetite is gone, I must be done for." I had to decide quickly on what was best to do; as I knew very well that if I died in my house the Councilors would burn it down on the pretext that it was infected. Just think of being mean and stupid enough to burn a new house for such a reason as that! But sooner than that should happen I would rather go out and die on my own dunghill. So, without losing a minute, I put on the worst old clothes I could find, made a bundle of a few books which I tied up with a chunk of bread and a candle, and told the apprentice to take a good holiday; then I locked the door of my house behind me, collected a few of my best books, and set off for a little place I had outside the town on the road to Beaumont, where I had built a little sort of shed or hut where I kept all sorts of rubbish, garden tools, a straw mattress, and a broken chair or two, "if they burn that," thinks I, "there will be no great harm done!"

I had not been there five minutes before I was in a high fever, my teeth chattered, I had a sharp stitch in my side, and my gizzard felt as if it was upside down. Now don't think for a moment, my friends, that at this painful moment I was heroic and endured my sufferings in the grand manner, like noble Romans in the history books. As I was all by myself with nothing near but the stomachache, I just threw myself down on my straw mattress and howled. You could have heard me as far as the big tree of Sembert.

"Good Lord," I groaned, "what pleasure can You take in tormenting a poor creature who never did You any harm? Oh, how my head aches! and my back feels as if it were broken. It is hard to be cut off in the flower of one's age and what difference can it make *when* I go to Heaven? — of course it would be a pleasure — an honor I mean, but why this indecent haste, since we are sure to meet sooner or later? I am perfectly willing to wait, for my part; a poor worm like me! Lord, if it is Your will, I am, as You see, resigned and humble but — oh, I can't bear these pains another minute!"

All this weeping and praying did not seem to do much good to my body, but it eased my mind a little, and as I became calmer I reflected that God was either deaf to my cries, or else that He did not choose to listen, which is much the same thing when you come to think of it. If man is made in His likeness, I thought, He will act as seems good to Him, so I may as well save my breath, for to all appearance what I have will not last more than an hour or two, so I will try and make the most of what is left in this dear old body, which I am reluctant to quit, even if it is to better myself. Well, we can die but once, so I may as well see how the thing is done, now that there is no help for it. When I was a little boy, I used to make willow-whistles, and I found the best way to loosen the bark was to tap it sharply with a knife-handle.

"Ah-h, I had a hard knock that time! The Lord no doubt is getting my bark off by the same method, but it does seem a strange sort of amusement for a Personage of His age, and there is nothing left for me but to watch and see what happens, which is hard when such a horrible commotion is going on inside one!" – [Here the author takes the liberty of omitting some lines, as Breugnon enters, with somewhat too much detail, into the disordered state of his machinery, which we fear would not be of interest to the general reader.] – There I lay reflecting, and sometimes stopping to howl a little, and at last I lighted my candle and stuck it in the neck of an old bottle, which smelt still of the spirit that once had filled it. "My body and soul will be like that by this time tomorrow," thought I, and then I turned over and tried to read a little, but the Romans and their lofty sentiments rather bored me, especially their self-satisfaction. "We are not all worthy to see Rome!" and sayings of that kind fell flat at that moment, when I had no pride left, and only wanted to complain of the cramp in my stomach.

When I had an interval of ease, however, I found such a good joke in an old jest book, that in spite of my aches and pains, I fairly roared with laughter, till it brought on the cramp again, and I had to stop and groan. Oh, what a night that was! When day dawned at last, I was really half dead, and could only drag myself on my hands and knees to the little window, where I called out in a lamentable voice to the first passerby I saw. One glance at me was enough. He made the sign of the Cross and fled for his life, and in fifteen minutes two sentinels were posted at my door with orders that on no account was I to cross the threshold. I could not have gone out if they had allowed it, but I begged them to go and fetch my old friend Paillard the notary, at Dornecy, so that I could make my will before dying. My guards were so afraid of the plague that they did not even dare to listen to the sound of my voice, but at last I found a messenger, a little boy whom I had caught one day stealing my cherries; he liked me because I told him he might as well pick some for me too while he was about it, so now he ran off on my errand.

I couldn't tell you what happened for a long time after that, I just lay all humped up on my mattress, burning with fever, but after a while I heard wheels on the road, and a familiar gruff voice, so I knew Paillard was there, and tried to raise myself and call to him. I wanted to tell him to draw up a codicil to my will leaving a larger share of my money to Martine and little Glodie, and in the long night I had thought out a way to do this so that my sons could not contest it. The great bell of St. Martin's seemed to be weighing on my forehead, but I managed to drag myself to the window, and out on the road I saw two round red faces staring at me with horror-stricken eyes. Paillard and Chamaille had rushed in hot haste to get a sight of their friend before he expired, but when they did see him, their ardor cooled a little, and they fell back so as to put the width of the road between us.

"Heavens!" cried Chamaille; "my poor friend, your color is something awful." But the mere sight of them seemed to restore me, so I called out, "You look hot, won't you come in and sit down a minute?"

"No, thank you, no!" they both said hastily; "we are all right out here," and they kept backing away towards the cart, where Paillard pretended to fumble with the bit of his old nag, to cover his embarrassment. Chamaille soon pulled himself together, for with him it was an everyday experience to talk with the dying; he first inquired how I was feeling, and when I said but poorly, he shook his head.

"Ah, my dear Colas!" said he sadly, "I have told you more times than I could count that this is what we must all come to; all flesh is grass, here today and gone tomorrow, but in the heyday of your youth you would never listen to me. Now alas! your cup is nearly empty, only the dregs remain to you, but all the same you ought not to be afflicted, since God does you the honor to summon you before Him, and I am here to prepare and wash your soul if perchance it is not perfectly clean and ready. Come, sinner, the time is short!"

"Vicar," said I, "I will attend to you in a few moments."

"The Chariot of Death will not wait for you."

"In that case I shall have to go on my two feet."

"Breugnon, my brother," said he solemnly, "relinquish your hold on the things of this world; why should you cling to them since they are naught but vanity and vexation of spirit?"

"Too true," said I, "and it breaks my heart to think of leaving old friends like you behind me in the midst of such desolation."

"We shall meet again!" said he, rolling up his eyes.

"Let it be soon then! You remember the motto of the Duke of Guise, 'Where I lead you follow!'"

"Come, come, Breugnon, time is passing, and so are you; do you want the father of lies to snap up your sinful soul for his dinner? He will, if you do not make your confession quickly, Colas! I entreat you for my sake!"

"For yours, for God's, and for my own sake," said I, "but first I have a word or two to say to the notary."

"Is it possible, Breugnon, that you will make the Eternal wait for the scrivener?"

"The Eternal has all eternity, so He will not mind waiting, besides it is more polite for me to take leave of this world which I am quitting, before I greet the next world where I am — perhaps — expected."

As I insisted in spite of all he could say to the contrary, Master Paillard took out his writing-case and sat down on a stone by the roadside, surrounded by a circle of spectators, and all the dogs in the neighborhood, while I dictated to him my last will and testament. Having disposed of my money, I turned my attention to my soul under the direction of Chamaille, till at last, feeling that my strength failed me, "Baptiste," said I, "your words are heavenly, but what avails the sky to a man whose throat is dry! Get me a stirrup-cup, for my soul is just about to spring to the saddle, so one bottle, if you love me!"

My last words fell on the willing ears of good neighbors and Christians who brought me not only one bottle but three, Chablis, Pouilly, and Irancy, and I, like a sailor setting out on a voyage, let down a rope out of my window; they put the wine in an old basket, tied the rope to its handle, and I pulled it up gently, my last best friend! After this, though the others had gone, I was not quite so lonely, but I kept no count of time, and could not tell now how the hours passed or rather how they seemed to be stolen from me, perhaps it was by the spirits in my trio of bottles, from which came voices and replies, but Colas Breugnon was not there to hear them.

Towards midnight I appeared to be seated in a strawberry bed looking up at the sky through the branches of a tree. How dark the earth was, and how the stars twinkled, the moon too was smiling at me, and all around were twisted distorted old stems and roots, like a nest of serpents grinning horribly. — What was I doing there? My head was spinning, but I seemed to say to myself, "Up with you, Colas! and lie no longer on that old mattress; the bottles are empty, out with you to the garden!" I wanted also to pick some cloves of garlic, because they are said to be a cure for the plague, but scarcely had I set foot on the ground when everything seemed to be enchanted; the sky arched over me like a huge tree, and from its drooping branches hung the stars like glittering fruit, and they all had eyes to look at me; they laughed, and so did the strawberries; high up among the leaves was a golden pear all ripe and juicy, and she sang in a sweet little voice:

> *"Grow like me*
> *From the tree,*
> *Little man below.*
> *Reach your hand to mine,*
> *Cling like stems of vine;*
> *Shake off all your woe,*
> *Grow with me*
> *As we upward go!"*

And the heavens and earth seemed like one big orchard full of fruits all singing, "Grow with me!"

Then I stuck my arms into the soft warm earth up to the elbows, and sank down till I was all enfolded from head to heel, as if on my mother's breast. From the July night rose the Song of Songs, the bright bunches of stars swung before my eyes, and the deep voice of St. Martin's struck the hour; twelve o'clock, fourteen, sixteen o'clock? Surely there was something strange in the old timepiece! And the star fruit above and below began to strike too, or was it chiming? with such celestial sounds that they pierced my heart, and vibrated in my ears like distant thunder. Then it seemed as I lay that a tree of Jesse was growing from me and I mounted with it, up, up among the chiming branches towards a bright planet dancing on the highest tree-top, and that I stretched out my arms to reach it, singing:

> "You are mine, Star wine,
> Spirit of the living vine, Halleluia!"

I must have kept on climbing for the greater part of the night, and from what they tell me I sang for hours, all sorts of songs, sacred and profane, some edifying and some very much the reverse; I also played on the dulcimer as well as on the drum and trumpet, till at last all the neighborhood came out to listen and to say, "Poor old Colas, he is dying, and mad as mad can be."

The next morning the sun was out of his bed long before I was, for I never opened my eyes till near midday, and my first thought was, "Good, here I am still living!" — not but what my couch was hard enough, and I still had those horrible pains in the gizzard, but I was glad enough that my body was there to put a pain in. "Breugnon, old man," said I, "it is a pleasure to see you; if you had died last night, I should never have got over it. Good-morning, dear garden, and everything in you!"

And while I was gloating on my beautiful melons, I heard some one hailing me from the other side of the wall. "Breugnon, are you dead yet?" And there were Paillard and Chamaille weeping and wailing, and prepared already to proclaim the virtues of the dear departed.

I crawled slowly from my bed, for my back was still confoundedly painful, and put my head gently out of the window. "Here he is," said I. "Cuckoo!"

"Colas!" they cried, laughing, while the tears ran down their faces, and I stuck out my tongue at them, telling them that I was not dead yet by a long sight, but if you will believe me those friends actually kept me shut up for ten days longer, till they were perfectly certain that I was entirely recovered. It is only fair to say that they kept me well supplied with bread and water, — I mean the kind that Noah drank, — and they came every day and sat under my window and told me all the news of town and country. When at last I was set free, Chamaille wanted me to go at once and return thanks to St. Roch, who according to him had delivered me from my mortal sickness. I told him I thought the saints that saved me had come out of three quart bottles.

"Well, Colas," said he, "we will split the difference, you come first with me to St. Roch and I will help you afterwards to render due thanks to St. Vineyard." So we made both these pious pilgrimages, all three together, for Paillard insisted on joining us.

"Friends," said I, "you were not so anxious to go with me the other day."

"You know I love you," said Paillard, "but I love my own self better, and as the proverb says, 'My skin fits tighter than my waistcoat.'"

"I am an old coward," said Chamaille, thumping himself on the chest, and looking very shamefaced.

"Well then," said I, "of what use are all the precepts of religion and of Cato?"

We all looked at each other and laughed. "Life is sweet," we cried, "and good men are scarce; if God thought fit to put us into this world, it is our duty to stay here as long as we can."

VIII
My Old Woman's Death

LIFE tasted good to me after my illness, better than ever before; the flavor of everything was enhanced, and I sat down to the world's table as Lazarus must have done, with a sharpened appetite. One day after hours, my foreman and I were in the shop amusing ourselves with a wrestling bout, when a neighbor looked in on his way from Morvan and told me that he had seen my wife there. I asked him how she was getting along. He said, "She was leaving when I saw her, making for a better world as fast as she was able."

"It won't be the better for her coming," said one would-be wit, and another cried, "Good luck never comes single; you stay with us, Colas, and she goes!" And he drank to my health.

I felt somewhat shaky, but not wishing to show it, I too held up my glass and answered, "When the gods love a man they take his wife away!" But I could not swallow the wine, it seemed tasteless, and suddenly starting up, I seized my stick and went out without saying another word. They called after me, but my heart was in my throat, and I could not answer. It was all very well to say that I did not love her, and that we had been constantly rubbing one another up the wrong way for the last thirty years; she had lain by my side in the narrow bed, and from her had sprung the seed I planted; and now that the pale shadow was near her, I felt a cold hand laid on my heart; it was as if a part of my flesh was torn from me, and though I had often wished to be rid of her, now I pitied her and myself, and — Heaven forgive me! — I almost loved her!

I arrived the next day at nightfall, and as soon as I came near my wife I could see on her face the hand of the great sculptor, and under the wrinkled skin the tragic mask of Death. There was a yet more certain sign, for she smiled as I came in, and said:

"Why, poor old man, I hope the walk has not tired you!"

Fancy her speaking to me like that! My heart sank, and I said to myself that there was no chance for her as I sat down by the bedside and took her hand in mine. Her eyes rested on me with affection, but she was too weak to talk, so I tried to cheer her up by telling all about my illness, and how I had got out of the clutches of the plague after all; but as it was the first she had heard of it the news proved almost too much for her, and she turned so faint that I was ready to beat myself on the head for my stupidity. However, she came to in a little while, and to my great relief began to scold me in her trembling voice; she was so weak that she could not get the words out fast enough, and it really did me good, and seemed like old times to be told that I ought to be ashamed of myself, that a man of any decency would have let his wife know when he caught the plague, and that I deserved to die of it all alone on my dunghill. The others were frightened at her violence, and wanted to send me out of the room, but I laughed and said that it would do her good to lose her temper, she was used to it; then I took her face in my two hands and kissed her on both cheeks, and will you believe it? the poor old thing began to cry.

For a long time after that I sat with her alone in silence, listening to the tick-tack of the death-watch in the wainscot; at last she tried to speak, but could only make a feeble murmur.

"Don't try to talk, old girl," said I. "I understand; we have not lived together thirty years for nothing."

"I have something I must say to you, Colas, or I should not rest easy in Paradise,—I have been very hard to you, my husband."

"No, no," said I, "only a bit sharp, and that was good for me."

"Yes, I was hard, jealous, quarrelsome; I know I often made the house too hot for you, but,—Colas, it was because I loved you!"

"You don't say so!" said I, patting her hand. "Well, there are all sorts of ways of loving, but yours was rather a queer one."

"I did love you," she went on, "and you never returned it, that was why I was cross, and you were always good-natured. Oh! that laugh of yours, Colas! You don't know how it made me suffer, till sometimes I really thought it would kill me. You covered yourself with it like a hood, and storm as I might, I could never get at you."

"My poor old dear!" said I; "that was because I do not like water!"

"There you go again laughing! But I don't mind it now that the chill of the grave is upon me; your laughter seems something warm and comforting, it does not anger me now,—and, Colas, say that you forgive me."

"You were an honest, hard-working, faithful wife to me," said I earnestly; "perhaps you were not always as sweet as sugar, but in this world, you know, one does not expect perfection, God keeps that for Himself up yonder; but when it came to hard times, you always backed me up. I used to think you really good-looking when I saw how you threw yourself into your work, whatever happened. Now I don't want you to torment yourself about the past, it's bad enough to have lived through it, but since it is all over, we might as well let the burden slip from our shoulders and cast all our cares on the Master. We have come to the end, and can take breath and look about us for a nice soft hole where we can sleep the sleep of the just which means, I suppose, of the good workers."

While I was talking, she lay with folded arms, and her eyes shut, and when I stopped she held out her hand. "Wake me tomorrow morning," she said. "And now good-night, my dear!"

Then she stretched herself out in the bed, and, neat as ever, she drew the sheet smoothly up to her chin, with the crucifix resting on her breast;—poor little woman, how thin she was! And there she lay, all ready, staring straight in front of her, waiting for the summons. It seemed that after so many years of effort her poor old body deserved some repose, but alas! there was one more trial in store for her. The landlady suddenly rushed into the room calling to me to come quickly, and when I did not at once understand, and told her to speak lower, it seemed as if the dying woman from her funeral couch could see beyond and above me, for she raised herself stiffly like him whom Jesus awakened, stretched out her arms, and cried, "Glodie!"

Her cry went through my heart, and as I heard a hoarse choking cough from the next room, I understood only too well, and ran in to find my poor little lark struggling with the croup, her cheeks all flushed and burning, as she put her hands up to her throat, and with wild eyes implored us to help her.

Oh, what a dreadful night that was! Even now a week later my knees give way under me when I think of it. Can it be that the Omnipotent causes the pain of such poor little creatures? How can He bear to see their eyes full of wondering reproach when it is in His power to save them? I can understand that since we are made in the image of our Creator, He may sometimes be cruel, as we are, or at least not always compassionate,—perhaps even capricious,—but grown-up men and women must set their teeth and take whatever comes to them, and they can always resist when things go too far, but that He should torment these helpless Iamblings is more than we can tolerate, and if this goes on, Lord, some day or other we shall withdraw our allegiance. If such crimes are possible it must be because You are blind, or else there is no Father up there!—Pardon, I must take that back, it is a little more than I intended. If You did not exist, I could not speak to You as I am doing, and we have had many a discussion, which always ended in my having the last word. —During the whole of that terrible night, I called to You, threatened, cursed, denied, implored You; clasped my hands in prayer, or shook my fist at You, but no voice came from above in answer, in spite of all I could do nothing seemed to touch You, till at last I cried out in desperation, "Lord, if You will not hear me, I will turn to some one less hard-hearted!"

Martine, the child's mother, had been taken with the pains of labor on her journey, and had been obliged to stop at Dornecy, leaving Glodie to the care of her grandmother; so now I had to watch alone with the old landlady. It seemed as if our little martyr would pass away with the night, and when dawn came I felt that there was but one thing left to do. Looking out I saw that it rained and a high wind blew through the doorway, but none the less, I made the sign of the Cross and lifted my darling from her pillow where she lay so exhausted that she had no further strength to struggle, but only panted a little like a bird in one's hand. She weighed no more than a feather as I carried her out, where a rose brushed against her in passing, — that's a sign of Death, they say, — but I crossed myself and went out sheltering her as best I could against the tempest. The landlady went first carrying presents, and so we came to the wood, where we found what we sought; a tall aspen standing high above the reeds on the edge of the swamp. Once, twice, three times we circled round the tree; the child lay quiet in my arms, only her teeth shook together like the leaves about us. We tied one end of a ribbon to her wrist, and fastened the other end to the aspen, and then the woman and I repeated this incantation:

> "Shake, shake,
> My sickness take.
> By the sweet Trinity,
> Thus do I order thee;
> But if thou reject my suit
> Ax shall soon destroy thy root."

Then the old woman dug a hole between the roots of the tree, in which she poured a pint of wine, and put in two cloves of garlic, a slice of bacon, and a copper penny; then we filled my hat with rushes, laid it on the ground, and again marched three times round it; the third time we spat in it and said, "Catch croup, cursed toads." Then we turned toward home, but near the edge of the wood we laid Glodie at the foot of a thorn tree, and put up a prayer to God's Son in the name of the Holy Thorn.

The little one was unconscious when we got back to the house, but we felt that we had done all we could; and it seemed too that my wife would not quit this world as long as Glodie remained in it. "Jesus, Mary," cried she, "I cannot go until I know that our child will recover, surely she must be cured, I swear it!"

Poor old dear, she was not as sure as she said, for she kept on praying, with a strength that astonished me when I remembered that I had thought her at her last breath the night before. "If that is the last, it is a good long one," said I, and was ashamed of myself for laughing at such a moment, but I could not help it. You cannot, of course, keep off suffering by laughter, but a Frenchman will always meet pain with a smile, and sad or merry you will find he has his eyes wide open; so, though I put a good face on it, my anxiety was as great as that of the poor old woman who was twisting and groaning in her bed. I tried to soothe her as we do children, tucking up the bedclothes which she had disordered; but she pushed me away, and told me that if I was worth my salt, I would do *something* for Glodie. "You cured yourself of the plague," said she, crying, "and yet you can do nothing for our darling! You are the one that ought to have died!"

"True enough, my dear, and I would give my skin to save her, but it is too old and cracked to be of use to anybody; all we are good for now is to suffer, the pair of us, and be as brave as we can, it may be some help to our little girl."

My wife leaned her head against mine, and our tears dropped together as we felt in the room the sweeping wings of the Archangel of Death.

All at once the sound of those great wings grew fainter, and as if by miracle hope dawned again. God had compassion on us, or the tender Jesus to whom I had prayed so fervently;—or else those elder gods of the earth and forest perhaps had heard our cries? Even our offering to the aspen may have helped us? But no matter what the reason, all we knew certainly was that from this moment the child's fever left her, once more she could draw her breath easily. Death had released her throat from the clutch of his pale fingers, she was given back to us! We did not know to whom we owed our thanks for this great mercy, but our hearts were filled with gratitude, and with tears of joy we sang "Nunc Dimittis," and then my poor old woman said, "Now I can go." She fell back on her pillow quite exhausted, the light in her eyes faded, her features grew sharp and hollow, and she sank down into the dark river, through which I could still seem to see the outline of her body;—until life was gone. I stooped and closed her eyelids, kissed her brow, and folded her workworn hands together for the rest they had never known till now, and turning from the extinguished lamp, I went to watch by the little flickering flame which was to be henceforward the light of my dwelling. Glodie slept, and as I sat by her side I could not help the thoughts that rushed over me:—Why is this little creature so unutterably dear that nothing seems worth while without her, and with her the worst that could happen would be bearable? Hers is the only life that matters; in comparison my own seems valueless, and yet here am I active of body and mind, with some talents, and what is even better, plenty of good sense; loving life, and made to enjoy it, in short a good Burgundian workman, and I would freely sacrifice all this for the sake of a little creature I do not even know; who is nothing as yet but a sweet face, a pretty plaything, but who will be something perhaps,—and for this possibility I am willing to give up my own "I am." Ah! it is because in this "perhaps "lies enfolded the fine flower of my existence, the best that is in me, and when I lie below the sod, and worms have destroyed this body, then will arise another self better and happier than the old one, yes, better, because I shall serve as a stepping-stone from which to see more clearly than I did.—You who are born of me, and will see the light when my eyes can no more behold it; through you I shall taste the vintage of the long future years, through you I shall enjoy the known and the unknown. All around me is passing as I shall pass, but you will lead me, ever farther and upward. I am no longer bound to my little holding here on earth; beyond my fields, beyond my life, the lines of the future stretch out into the infinite; they cover the years to come as the Milky Way covers the night sky. I have sown the seed of future harvests, and in you who will live after me I put my desire and my eternal hope.

IX
The Fire

15th of August.

I CAN hardly bear to tell of what happened today, and I feel as if I could never really reconcile myself to it; but as I always say, "Cheer up, Colas! a brave heart will carry you through everything." I have often heard it said that summer's rain gives no pain; but you would agree that it gives no gain, either, if you could see me after a season when one storm after another has beat on my devoted head; here I am without shoes or shirt to cover me, — but let me tell you all about it. — I was just pulling myself together after a double trial, you remember? Glodie had been cured of the croup and my poor wife of all the troubles of this world; when a fresh blow fell on me at the hands, I suppose, of the heavenly powers, — unless there is some woman up there who has a grudge against me? — but this time I am stripped to the skin, and glad enough to have that left on my bones. I had been in no hurry to come home while Glodie was recovering from her illness; a child's convalescence is so charming!

It is as if one saw a fresh creation, everything looks smooth and white like a new-laid egg; and as I had little to do, I went to market by way of amusement, and just to know what was going on in the world. One day I heard something which made me prick up my ears like an old mule. They said that a great fire was raging at Clamecy, that it had spread to the suburb of Beuvron, and that the whole place was burning up like a bundle of kindling wood. Naturally I asked eagerly about my own house, but could hear nothing further, and felt as if I was on hot coals, — probably from association of ideas, — though all my friends tried to calm me by saying that my house could be in no danger, or I should have heard of it by this time, that ill news travels fast, and that I was certainly not the only fool in Beuvron.

In spite of all this a voice told me that my house was on fire; — I could almost smell it, and without further words I started off, thinking as I went how careless I had been, to leave everything at sixes and sevens. Other conflagrations had been caused by the enemy, and I always had had warning enough to transport my most precious possessions across the bridge, and get them behind walls, so that I saved my money, my best pieces of work, furniture and tools, and all those things that people accumulate, and which are dear to us because they are like fragments of a happy past. This time, however, nothing had been placed in safety, and I could almost hear my old woman's voice from the other world, berating me for my stupidity. As I trudged along, I tried to find a good answer to these reproaches, but my only excuse was that I had been in a hurry to get to her sick-bed. I endeavored to persuade myself also, that there was no real cause for alarm, but the thought kept coming back and back, like a fly that settles on your nose, till I was all in a cold perspiration, in spite of the fact that I was walking at a good round pace. As I climbed up the long wooded hill just after you pass Villiers, I saw a chaise coming down; I could not tell who was driving at first, but when it got nearer, I recognized Jojot, the miller from Moulot.

He pulled up as soon as he caught sight of me.

"Poor old boy!" he cried, waving his whip, and though I expected it, the wind was just knocked out of me, and I could not say a word, but stood there like a stick, with my mouth open.

"There is no use in your keeping on, Colas; you might as well go back where you came from. The whole thing is burned, flat as the palm of your hand; it will only make you sick to see it." Every word seemed to wring my heartstrings, but I tried to put a good face on it, and said:

"I know, I know, but I must go on all the same."

"What for, if the whole place is in ruins?"

"I want to pick up the pieces."

"There aren't any pieces," said he, "not so much as you could put on the end of your finger."

"Jojot," said I, "there is no use your trying to persuade me that there is absolutely nothing left! My apprentices and the neighbors would not stand by, and see all I have in the world burnt to ashes, without trying to save a few sticks of furniture for me!"

"You don't know anything about it," cried he. "Why, your neighbors are the very ones who set your house on fire!"

I was perfectly crushed at this news, and he, with the sort of perverse satisfaction one has in making out anything as bad as possible, went on to tell me the whole story from the beginning.

"You must know," said he, "that the plague is at the bottom of the trouble; our town Councilors, the Provost, and the whole crew of them, fled away, and left us as sheep without a shepherd, and the people at this lost their heads completely, so that when a fresh case of the disease broke out in Beuvron, some one raised a cry to burn down the infected houses. No sooner said than done, and naturally they began with yours, Colas, because you were not on hand to stop them. The more they burned, the better they seemed to like it; you know how a mob is when it once gets going, men seem to be drunk with love of destruction, so they went on from bad to worse, as if they were crazy; throwing everything they could lay hands on into the flames, and dancing round them like savages.

"On the bridge of Clamecy town,
See us dancing up and down."

you know the children's song. It was really awful to see such madness, and yet it was a kind of contagion. I'll bet you would have danced yourself if you had been there, to see what a blaze your shop made with all the dry wood you had in it."

"I wish I had been there," said I. "It must have been a grand sight."

And the funny part of it was that I really did think so. I thought something else too: that this time I was ruined; but wild horses would not have dragged it out of me before Jojot. He was puzzled, and looked as if he did not know what to make of me, half with that queer pleasure we have in the misfortunes of our fellow-man, and half with pity, for he is really a good sort, and a friend of mine. I turned to go.

"They ought to have kept a thing like that for the midsummer bonfire," said I.

"Are you really going on?"

"Yes, I'm going on, Jojot."

"Well, you're an odd fish — you do hate to be like other people." And he whipped up his horse and drove off down the hill, while I stepped out bravely in the opposite direction as long as he was in sight; but as soon as I got round the corner, my knees seemed to give way under me, and I let myself fall like a lump by the roadside.

The next moments were among the worst that I have ever had to bear, and as there was nobody to see me, I just let myself go, and bewailed my misfortune.

"I have lost everything in the world," thought I. My home, — the house was full of dear memories, — and the hope of ever having another of my own; all my savings, which it took me years to get together, bit by bit, and which were so much the more valuable to me, and worst of all, my independence is gone; for now of course, I shall have to live with one of my children, and I don't know which of us will hate it the most. It is the one thing I have always been resolved against, as the worst that could happen. There is no use telling me that I love them, and they love me, — I know all that, but young people and old interfere with each other, and it is natural and proper for a bird to sit on its own nest, and hatch out its own eggs in its own way. Respect for the old is all very well, or rather it makes a difficulty, for you are not on an equality with people when you are obliged to show them respect. I have tried to behave so that my five children should not have too much respect for me, and I think I have succeeded pretty well, but there must always be a distance between us. Parents come and go in their children's lives, like strangers from a far country; there can never be perfect understanding from one generation to another, and too often there is, on the contrary, interference and irritation.

It seems a dreadful thing to say, but it is not wise to tempt Providence, and put too great a strain on the love, even of our best and dearest. It is asking a great deal of human nature; not that I have anything to complain of in my children, who have always been good to me, but I don't want to impose myself on them, for my own sake, as well as theirs; — and then it goes against the grain with me to take back the least part of what I have given them; it looks like asking for repayment, and that is a sort of thing that sticks in the throat of a man who has never owed anything to anybody but himself. I want to be master in my own house, to come and go without question; and it would kill me to think that some one was counting every mouthful I ate; I should soon become a broken-down, good-for-nothing old man. Far rather would I live on the charity of strangers than on that of my children, never being sure that they kept me of their own free will. I would rather die outright than be such a burden to them. ... I sat there for a long time, like an old tree that has been cut down at the roots; and there was precious little of my boasted philosophy left. I suffered in my pride, and in my affections; in what was best and worst in me; accumulations from the past, and hopes for the future, had all gone up in smoke, but I knew that I must walk in the path before me, however thorny it might prove; there could be no escape.

Not far off above the tops of the trees, my sad eyes lighted on the towers of the Château of Cuncy, and I felt that there they had found something on which they might rest with pleasure. For many years I had worked for the good lord Philibert de Cuncy; and the castle was full of fine furniture, woodwork, and stairways, which I had executed at his order. He was a queer man, and I sometimes got into hot water with him. Would you believe it? once he wanted me to make portrait statues of his mistresses and himself all in costumes dating from the days of Adam and Eve! Another time he took it into his head to have the stag's antlers in his armory attached to busts representing all the unlucky husbands in the vicinity. We had a good laugh over it, but it was not always so easy to please him; as fast as I finished one thing, he wanted me to begin another, and very seldom did I see the color of his money. Never mind! he was a genuine lover of art, and of woman, and much in the same way too. In this I was much of his mind, for I have always thought a man should love a work of art, as he does his mistress, with the flesh as well as the spirit.

It was a consolation to me to think that so much of my best work survived, now that the rest had perished, even if it was not paid for; and I felt a longing to go and see the fruit of my past labors, hoping that it might make life seem less hard to me. At the castle I was well known, and they let me go where I would. The Master was away, they said, but I told them I had some measurements to take for new work, and I knew where to find the children of my brains and my fingers, though it was some time since I had seen them. As long as an artist feels in himself the power of fresh creation, he does not care to dwell on his former productions, and besides, the last time I was here, the Master had made some excuse to prevent my coming in. I thought at the time, that he looked rather queer, but suspected perhaps that he was hiding some married woman, and as I was quite sure it was not my wife, I thought no more about it; besides, no one at Cuncy ever pays much attention to the Master's vagaries; he is a little cracked, they say, and let it go at that.

I had not mounted ten steps of the staircase before I was struck motionless, like Lot's wife, by the sight which met my eyes. The fine carving which ran along the banisters, representing vines and flowering branches, was all hacked and disfigured so that I could hardly believe it, and had to touch and feel the rough edge to convince myself that these injuries had been made deliberately with a knife or hatchet. My breath came short, and I trembled to think of what yet might be in store for me, but I took the rest of the stair four steps at a time, and burst open the great doors on the landing. As I looked down the long range of apartments, I saw that my worst fears were realized. In the armory, the dining-hall, and the state bedroom, my beautiful little figurines had all been mutilated, shorn of their noses, their arms, or their legs. Silly inscriptions, names or dates, were cut deep in the panels of the wardrobes, on the chimney breasts, or across the fluted pilasters. At the head of the long gallery stood a charming group, — a nymph of the Yonne, with her bare knee on the neck of a shaggy lioness. This they had used as a target, so that it was all battered by shots from an arquebus. Some of the faces were ornamented with mustaches, or had low jokes scrawled upon them with wine stains or ink. Everywhere were gashes, chips, or rubbish; all that loneliness, idleness, or stupidity could suggest to the mind of a rich idiot, on the lookout for some new amusement, destruction and disfigurement being the only things that could come into the head of a creature too dull to be of any use himself in the world. It is lucky that he was not there, for in the first transport of rage I believe that I should have killed him. I could not speak at first, but the veins of my neck swelled up, and my eyes started from my head like a lobster's. Another moment, and I really should have burst! but fortunately I managed to let out an oath or two, and then my rage came in a flood, and I screamed, stamped, and swore like a man demented.

"Dog! beast! ruffian!" cried I. "I gave you these lovely children of my art, to ornament your vile den, and look what you have done to them! I thought that they would adorn your house and carry on my name for generations, and here they are, spoiled, tortured, and violated! What joy was mine when I evoked all these from the enduring wood, and worked with loving care to make them beautiful, perfect in every limb, — and now see them, thus soiled and mutilated from head to foot, defaced and ruined. Poor dears! your own father scarcely knows you, one would think that you had all been to the wars!"

And then I put up a fervent prayer to Heaven (which was perhaps superfluous), entreating that I might not enter Paradise, but be sent to the nethermost hell, where I might assist Lucifer in tormenting my enemy. "Ah!—ha! when I think of this brutal destroyer, how I should love to stick a spit through him and twirl him before a slow fire!"

The steward Andoche came in, while I was still foaming with rage; he begged me as an old acquaintance to calm myself, and led me from the room, saying what he could to console me.

"They are only bits of wood, after all," he said. "It is not worth while for you to excite yourself so for things like that; and what would you do if you had to live here, like us, with this lunatic? If he wants to knock anything about,—and after all a man must have some pleasure,—why should he not kick these chunks of wood, for which you got a fair price, instead of good Christians like you and me?"

"I don't care how much he beats you," said I. "I had rather have been flogged myself than have had him injure this wood into which I had breathed the breath of life. Do you think a man cares for his bones? It is his thought that is sacred to him, and he who kills that is thrice guilty!" Carried away by my own eloquence, I might have kept on like this for hours, but I saw that Andoche did not grasp a word of it, and indeed seemed to think that I was nearly as cracked as his Master. I turned on the threshold and gave a last look, as one may say, at the field of battle, where lay my poor noseless creations; there was Andoche with his pitying smile, and here was I wasting my breath in cursing at these dummies. It struck me all at once as so deucedly funny, that I just laughed in Andoche's face, and went off in a gust of merriment which seemed to carry away my anger and my pain along with it.

I struck out towards Clamecy, musing as I went, "This time," thought I, "they may as well stick me under ground; for there is nothing left of the old man but his skin. Hold on, though, there may be something worth while inside of that,—I remember a story of a fellow who was besieged, and they told him to yield, or they would kill all his children. He answered that if they did, he knew how to make a lot of new ones. That is my position exactly. In the dry places of the earth we artists have sown grain which wild beasts and birds of the air come to devour, because they do not know how to create, and can only feed on the works of others; but let them trample and uproot as much as they will, I have a store from which I can replenish the fruitful soil. Let the wheat ripen or die, it does not matter, for my eyes are fixed, not on the past, but on the future, and when the day comes, as it will, when none are left to me of all my members, when the sight of my eyes is dimmed, and my hands have lost their cunning, then when that time comes, Colas, you will have ceased to be. Is it possible to imagine a Breugnon, who cannot work or feel, who does not laugh or spring from the ground with both feet at once? No, then he will be only a withered nut, you can throw the old shell into the fire!"

I was so much comforted by these reflections that when I reached the top of the last hill as you go towards Clamecy I went on gaily, throwing my feet out, and twirling my stick with a jaunty air, when I saw in the distance a boy running towards me, seemingly in much distress. As he came nearer, I knew him for my youngest apprentice, a lad about thirteen years old, Robinet, called Binet; certainly as idle a youngster as ever stared out of a window at the girls, when he should have been hard at work. Twenty times a day I had to cuff him for his laziness, but he was a clever little monkey, and his agile fingers could turn out astonishingly good things when he liked; and then his funny face with its wide mouth and turned-up nose, was so attractive that, for the life of me, I could not be really angry with him. He knew it, the young rascal! and when I hit him a good clip, he would just shake his ears like a donkey, and in ten minutes was as bad as ever.

Imagine my surprise when I saw that he was crying, the large drops streaming in rivulets down his cheeks, and before I could say a word, he flung his arms round my neck, blubbering, and bedewing me with his tears, like a Triton in a fountain.

"Stand off!" cried I. "What on earth is the matter with you? And, for goodness' sake, blow your nose, first, if you want to kiss me!"

Then as I saw that, far from stopping, he let himself slip to the ground and lay there, sobbing louder than ever, I became really alarmed, and raised him, so that I saw that one hand was wrapped in a bloody rag, that his eyebrows were singed, and his clothes torn and dusty.

"Come, my boy, what is the matter? What mischief have you been up to this time?" — I had really forgotten my disaster.

"Oh, Master! — the fire! I can't bear to tell you," said he, weeping, and when I realized that the poor child was unhappy on my account, because my house was burned down, I cannot tell you what a comfort it was to me.

"My poor boy!" said I, "don't cry any longer."

He thought that I had not understood, and told me more calmly that my workshop and my house were burned to the ground.

"That's an old story by now," said I, patting him on the back. "You are the fourth or fifth person who has told me of it. Well! it's hard luck, that's all I can say, but I never thought you cared so much about the old shop. Honor bright, now, didn't you dance around it, like the others, while it was burning?"

The way I was taking it had made him feel much better, but at this he shook off my hand indignantly. "You don't believe a word of it, Master; Cagnat and I did all we could to put it out, but there were only two of us, and Cagnat was sick with the fever; he got out of his bed to help, and we tried to hold the door of the house against the crowd, but what was the use? They threw us down, and trampled us under foot like a herd of wild cattle! We were swept off our feet as if a flood had gone over us, and when Cagnat managed to pick himself up, and tried to prevent them from setting fire to the house, they very nearly killed him.

"I got into the workshop somehow, though it was already in a blaze, flaming like a torch from top to bottom, with long red banners of fire streaming from the roof and windows. The smoke nearly choked me, and I thought I should be burnt to a crisp, but I made one bound into a heap of shavings, which were so hot that they set my breeches on fire, and it did not take me long to jump out of them again. I hit my head such a crack on the corner of the workbench that it half stunned me, but not for long; all around the fire was crackling and roaring, and outside I could hear the cries of those mad devils.

"I crawled on my hands and knees towards your figure of St. Marie Madeleine, which I saw near me; I could not bear to see the flames licking up over her little rounded body, and her long beautiful hair!— I just jumped at her, beat out the sparks with my fingers, and caught her in my arms as if she had been alive. 'Dear St. Madelon! treasure of my heart,' cried I, 'don't be afraid, I will save you,—and myself too, if I have luck!' There was not a minute to spare, for by this time the roof was falling in, and I could not get out the way I came. But I spied the round loophole in the wall towards the river, struck the glass a blow with my fist, and jumped through it with my saint, as if it had been a paper hoop! A tight fit, I can tell you! but out we popped, splash, to the bottom of the Beuvron! Luckily the bottom is not far from the top, and very soft and muddy, so Madeleine did not so much as bump her pretty head, but as I had not the sense to let go of her, she dragged me down face first, till I was so full of slime and river water that it was a hard job to pull myself out with the lady. So here we are, at last, Master, and I only wish that I could have saved more for you!"

He had a bundle under his arm wrapped up in an old waistcoat, and when he carefully unrolled it, I saw the sweet face of my little saint, not much the worse, except for her scorched toes. Up to this time I had not wept for all the misfortunes that had fallen on me, but at the sight I was touched to the quick, and taking Madeleine and the boy in my arms, I kissed them both, and cried, till the tears ran down my cheeks.

"What became of Cagnat?" I asked when I had recovered myself a little, and reading the answer in the boy's face, I knelt down, and put my lips to the earth in honor of a brave spirit.

"God reward you both!" I cried, as I looked at the lad still clasping the statue in his bandaged arms, and I thought, "These will last, the souls of these children, on which I have wrought my impress;—wood and stone may be destroyed, but this joy no man can take from me!"

X
The Riot

August 30.

WHEN we were a little calmed down, I said to Robinet, "What is done is done, let us see now what is before us." For I always think that the best way to act in the present is to look upon yesterday's doings as ancient history. I had been away from Clamecy about three weeks, and I made him sit down and tell me all that had happened in the interval. The town had been under a double curse, the plague and fear, and when the pestilence abated, fear seemed the more dangerous. Bandits flocked from all the surrounding country, to prey upon the unfortunate place; the people were so terrified that they offered no resistance, and those of the baser sort, driven out their wits by fright, even joined themselves to the robbers.

The law had become a dead letter, for of our four Aldermen, one died, two fled, and the Public Prosecutor had also bolted. The Commandant at the Citadel was brave enough, but old, and crippled by gout, besides, having no more brains than you could put in a thimble, he had allowed himself to be torn in pieces.

The only official that remained in the town was the fourth Alderman, a man named Racquin, who finding himself deserted by his colleagues, and opposed by this raging mob, was weak, or cunning enough, to yield to it, instead of trying to put a stop to its depredations. He even allowed the mob to set fire to the houses of men against whom he had a grudge for one reason or another, myself among the number.

"What are the citizens doing all this time?" I asked.

"Nothing, now that their leaders are gone; they are like lambs led to the slaughter."

"Well, how about me, Binet? This old ram has some fight left in him still, so come along!"

"You are crazy, Master! What could you do, one man, against hundreds of brigands?"

"Do? — the best I can, of course; why should I be afraid of robbers, now that I have not a penny left in the world? Come on, I say."

Now, would you believe it? that boy actually turned a handspring on the road for joy, in spite of his burned hand, and bruises, and began to dance about and shout that this was the greatest sport he had ever heard of.

"Hooray!" he cried; "we'll chase these beggars off the face of the earth!"

"Stop! you young monkey," said I. "You'll be swinging soon, perhaps, by your neck instead of by your tail, so keep still, and mind what I tell you.... I'm off for Clamecy now by myself, and you must make the best of your way to Dorncey. When you get there, find Magistrate Nicole, our alderman. He thought it prudent to run, I know, but he is kind-hearted, even if he does love himself better than his neighbor, and there are things he prizes still more,—viz.: his goods and chattels, which are in the greatest peril, as you will not fail to tell him.

"When you have seen him, push on to Sardy, to Master Courtignon, the Procurator; you'll find him in his house with a pigeon-cote there; let him know that his mansion in Clamecy, with all it contains, will be burnt to the ground this very night, unless he comes back;—that will fetch him, I promise you! But I don't need to give you lessons in lying, you young rascal! I'll be bound you know well enough what to say to them."

"Oh! I don't mind a lie or two, but the fact is, Master, I would rather not leave you alone."

"As if a snip like you would be of any protection! Seriously, Binet, the best thing you can do for me is to get help, so hurry off as fast as you can, and when you have done my errand, join me at the town."

"Old Courtignon and Nicole shall be brought back," he cried, "if I have to drag them here by the hair of their heads; but just tell me one thing, Master,—what are we going to do with them when they get here?"

"You will see," said I with an air of profound mystery, though I knew myself no more than the babe unborn what was to be the outcome. The sun had set in a bank of red clouds, and the lovely summer evening was closing in when I got to the town about eight o'clock; but fine as it was, there was not a soul about; no guards and no loungers outside the market gate; so I walked boldly up the High Street, where the only living thing I met was a half-starved cat, which fled when it saw me. The houses, all tightly closed, turned blind eyes on the street, with doors and windows barred; and the only sound I heard was the echo of my own footsteps.

"I am too late," I said to myself, "they are all dead." Just then I thought I heard a rustling behind the shutters, so I banged on the nearest door and shouted, "Let me in!" Getting no answer I tried another house and another, rattling the handles and knocking loudly with my stick, but not a door was opened. I could hear faint noises inside as if mice were stirring, and I understood that the miserable cowards were all hiding. This made me so angry that I cried out, "Denis Saulsoy, old man, if you don't open the door, I'll beat it down! It is I, Breugnon."

At my name all the shutters flew open as if by magic; and I saw a row of frightened faces all along Market Street, like a lot of onions lying on the window sills. They stared at me as if I were the most beautiful thing in creation, and as the terror faded from their eyes, they looked so pleased that I flattered myself that it was from affection for me; but the fact was, the sight of any one there at that hour was reassuring. Then ensued a very interesting dialogue between Breugnon and the onions; they all talked at once, and I replied as best I was able. They wanted to know where I came from, what I was doing, where I was going, how I got in, and how I meant to get out? To which I answered that I was glad to find that their tongues were still in working order, though their courage seemed somewhat rusty.

"I want to talk to you," I cried. "Come out! It is a charming evening, what are you all sticking in the house for, — has somebody stolen your breeches?"

"Breugnon," they said in a frightened whisper, "did you see any one in the streets?"

"Whom did you expect to see, idiots?"

"The brigands; they are burning everything in Béyant."

"Why don't you go and stop them then, you fools?"

"We have to stay here to protect our houses."

"The best way to protect your own houses is to go out and fight for other people's; don't you see that when the brigands have burnt down the rest of the houses, they will take yours? Your time will come, never fear!"

"Master Racquin told us that the best thing we could do was to keep quiet till order was reestablished by the Duke of Nevers."

"A lot of water will run under the bridges before the Duke leaves his own business to look after ours; we shall all be burned to a cinder by that time. Come, come! We ought to fight for our skin, if it is worth anything."

They kept on for some time making objections, chirping like birds from window to window, declaring that the enemy was numerous and powerful, and that we were weak and had no one to lead us; till I lost all patience, and swore that I would not stand there in the street any longer gaping at them.

"Do you think I am here to serenade you?" I cried. "Let the women stay up there, to take care of your houses, they are quite equal to that. But if there are any men among you, come down and fight, or, by the God that made me, I will set fire to you myself with my own hands!"

At last one braver than the rest stuck his nose out of the door, half laughing, and then they all came out one after the other, and stood round me in a circle.

"Are you quite cured of the plague?"

"As right as a trivet."

"And has no one attacked you?"

"Only a lot of geese, but who cares for their hissing? Listen, my friends, you see I am here all safe and sound; don't you think that there has been enough of all this nonsense? It is time to go to work, and now, some of you tell me where we can go to plan for what must be done."

"You can come to my forge, if you like," said Gangnot, and led the way; soon we were all gathered there in the darkness, with the door tight shut. The place smelt of burnt horn and horses, and a lantern standing on the rough floor threw our monstrous shadows on the smoky beams of the roof. At first no one dared to speak a word, and then they all broke out and talked at once, until Gangnot seized his great hammer and struck a resounding blow on the anvil, which shook the loud voices again into silence; whereupon I managed to make myself heard.

"Friends," said I, "don't waste your breath in telling me what has happened, for I know as much as you do about it;—you say the brigands are here,—I say we must throw them out; you say the mob is on their side,—well, what of that? Mobs are men, just like you and me, who want to wet their throats when they see others drinking. We are told it is a sin to tempt Providence, but it is still worse to dangle a lot of rich booty before the eyes of poor devils, who have not one penny to rub against another; they may not be thieves themselves, but they have no objection to profit by the stealings of others. You know, there are all sorts of people in the world, and as the Lord says, we must divide the sheep from the goats."

"Master Racquin is an Alderman, and he ordered us to do nothing," said some of the more timid. "The whole authority of the city rests in his hands, you know, and now that the Lieutenant, the Procurator, and all the others are absent, he is charged to keep order."

"Well, does he do it?"

"He tries his best."

"I ask you, has he kept the town in order? No! Well then, we will do it ourselves!"

"Master Racquin has solemnly promised us that if we keep perfectly quiet, all our property shall be protected, and the disturbances be confined to the suburbs."

"And how is he going to keep that promise?"

"He was forced to make some kind of a treaty with the brigands, but he says that it was only to get them in his power."

"To hoodwink us, you mean,—why, such a treaty is a positive crime!"

They all hung their heads, looking angry and shamefaced as well as frightened, and Denis Saulsoy said quickly, timidly, that it was not safe always to speak out what one thought. Gangnot was a man of few words, but he gave the anvil another blow, and said, "Colas is right!"

"What are you afraid of, Denis?" said I. "You are among friends,—do you think that walls have ears? Here, Gangnot, go and stand in front of the door with that hammer of yours, and knock the head off the first man that tries to enter; he may have ears to listen with, but I bet that he won't have a tongue to wag, after Gangnot has had a good lick at him! Now is the time to decide; speak up, if you are true men, for when we leave here it will be to act, not to talk."

This brought them all to their feet in a perfect uproar; they broke out in a storm of rage against Racquin, calling him a rascal, and Judas, and swearing that he had sold us outright and all that we possessed; but since he had the police behind him, they were afraid to move or offer any resistance.

"Where is he to be found?" said I.

They told me, at the Town Hall, where he stayed night and day, guarded by a troop of ragamuffins, who were more like jailers than defenders.

"He is a prisoner then, in a word," cried I. "Gangnot, open that door! We will go at once and set him free; — who is with me? It is too late to hang back now!"

"Breugnon," said Saulsoy, scratching his head, "I do not mind a few hard knocks, but it is a different matter to go against a man who represents the law; if you resist the law, you are taking a heavy —"

"Res-pon-si-bil-i-ty!" said I. "Well, why not? My shoulders are broad enough to bear it, so none of the rest of you need worry. When I see a scoundrel I kill him first, and find out afterwards if he is Pope or Procurator. When order has turned to chaos, it is time to take the law into our own hands."

This ended the discussion, and we all filed out with Gangnot at our head, his hammer in his huge four-fingered hand, (he had crushed one of them on the anvil). He looked like a walking tower, tall and strong, his face blackened by smoke, and one eye squinting horribly, but we all crowded in behind his broad back, and each man ran to his house to get his weapons. I should not like to swear that they all came back armed; perhaps some of the poor fellows could not find their axes or their arquebuses, for when we assembled in the marketplace, our ranks were rather thin, if the truth were told; but those who did come were true as steel; men you could put your trust in.

When we got to the Town Hall, we found by great good luck that the main door was wide open; perhaps because our kind shepherd was so sure that his lambs would let themselves be shorn without so much as a baa-a, that he and his watch-dogs, having partaken of a hearty dinner, were all wrapped in slumber. Under these circumstances our assault was by no means heroic; we just walked in, and caught, as they say, the bird on her nest.

Racquin was dragged out of his bed, just as he was, like a skinned rabbit; and he looked anything but pretty, with rolls of fat all over his pink body, even on his forehead and round his eyes. We soon found that he knew what we were after, and was equal to the situation. He flashed an angry glare at us out of his sharp gray eyes, under their puffy eyelids; but he controlled himself at once, and with an authoritative air, inquired by what right we thus invaded the precincts of the law. I answered that we only wanted to drag him out of bed. This made him furiously angry, but Saulsoy said to him, "Master Racquin, you are not the one to threaten us; the boot is on the other leg now. We are here to accuse you, so defend yourself if you can."

He changed his tune at once. "Fellow-citizens," said he blandly, "what would you have of me? What complaint do you bring? I have stayed in the town to protect you at the risk of my own life, when all my brother officials fled before the plague and the riots. I alone have remained faithful at my post. The evils which have come upon you are surely none of my causing, so what fault can any of you find with me?"

"You are the physician of the town, Racquin," said I, "and as the proverb says, 'Clever doctors make bad sores.' — You have fattened on the plague and the riots, you and your creatures; you are in league with the robbers to burn down our houses, which you ought to protect; and instead of resisting the mobs, you have made yourself a leader among them. We do not know if you have thus betrayed us through fear or greed, but you shall choose yourself what label we are to hang about your neck: 'This is one who sold his town for thirty pieces of silver.' Prices are higher than they were in Iscariot's day, so I will put instead, 'An Alderman who saved his own skin at the expense of his fellow-citizens.'"

"Breugnon," said he, with an ugly look, "I have only done my duty in burning infected dwellings according to law."

"Yes, and when a man is not one of your adherents you mark his house with a cross, and call it infected. And how about letting the mob in to pillage? That is a good way to stop the spread of the plague, isn't it?"

"I was unable to prevent it, in all cases, and besides, if these ruffians catch the pest while they are looting the houses, so much the better, we are rid of two nuisances at once."

"A splendid idea. The robbers kill the plague, and the plague kills the robbers, and the Alderman inherits what remains of the town! It is as I said just now, the clever doctor survives both disease and patient. Now I tell you what it is, Master Racquin, your treatment is too high-priced for us. We will take care of ourselves from this time onward, and by way of salary for former services, we will give you — "

"Six feet of ground in the nearest graveyard," Gangnot finished the sentence for me, and at the word our followers sprang forward like a pack of wolves. I threw myself before their prey, while he took refuge between the bed and the wall, staring wildly out at their furious faces. He was such a miserable object, shivering there like a fat pig, without a rag to cover him that, just out of pity, I told him to get his clothes on.

"We have seen enough of your hide, for one while, my friend," said I. This made the others laugh, and seeing them in a better humor, I began to try to make them hear reason. Racquin meanwhile hurried on his clothes, his teeth chattering with cold, and an evil gleam in his eye. He knew that the danger was over for the moment; that for a day at least his life was reasonably safe, so when he was fully dressed, he plucked up his courage and went so far as to call us all rebels; threatening to punish us for insulting a magistrate.

"You are no longer Magistrate," said I. "You are dismissed by my order!"

At this he turned on me; forgetting all prudence, and screaming with rage, he cried out that he knew me for a rascally trouble-maker; that I had stirred up the others to attack him, and that on me should fall the most condign punishment.

"Shall I kill him?" said Gangnot, balancing his hammer. I held him back as I answered:

"It is lucky for you, Racquin, that I have been ruined, for you know well enough that, if I hanged you now, people would say it was out of revenge for the fire. A halter would just suit your style of beauty, and one of these days you will certainly wear one round that fat neck of yours. But the thing is that we have got you now, and are going to strip your Alderman's gown from your back; we are the Government here until further notice."

"You are taking your life in your hand, Breugnon."

"What if I am? I risk it for the good of the town, and if I lose, Clamecy will be the winner!"

He was sent to prison forthwith, and to make room for him we released an old sergeant whom he had shut up three days before, for disobedience of orders. The sheriff and all of the staff at the Town Hall came round to our side, now that the blow was struck, declaring that Racquin was a traitor, and that they had always said so; (if they had, it was in a very low whisper).

Our plan had run as smoothly as if on wheels, up to now; so much so that I was really surprised, and asked, "Where on earth are the brigands?" And just then a breathless messenger ran up to warn us that the mob was outside the Lourdeaux gate-tower, and that they were attacking Peter Poullard's warehouse in Béyant, burning, sacking, and carrying all before them.

"This time," said I, "they will have to dance to our piping," and we rushed down to the Mirandole terrace, which overhangs the lower town. We could see nothing but a dense cloud of smoke shot through with red flames; above our heads sounded the frantic tocsin from the tower of St. Martin's, while from below rose a perfectly infernal clamor.

"Comrades," said I, "let us get down there as quick as we can, for the oven is heating, and no mistake, — but who is to lead us? You, Saulsoy?"

He hung back, however, saying that it was bad enough to be out of his bed at midnight, with an old musket in his hand, but when it came to making him Captain, that was a little too much! He did not mind obeying, he said, but for a fellow who had never been able to decide anything in his life, it was ridiculous to ask him to give orders.

"Who will be chief, then?"

No one stirred; I was ready to dance with impatience, but such people are all alike, willing enough to follow, but when it comes to taking the lead, no one at home! They were all cautious householders, and with them the habit of hesitation is so inveterate that they will spend half a day bargaining over the sheet they want to buy, and fingering the linen until, perhaps, the chance is gone.

"If no one else offers, I will be captain!" cried I. "But first understand one thing: for this night I give orders and you obey them; no talking, no hanging back, for if we fail now we are all lost; so remember I am to be master. It will be time enough to judge me tomorrow. What do you say?"

"Agreed!" they shouted with one voice, and we started down the hill. I went first, Gangnot at my left, and Bardet, the town crier, on my right with his drum. Down by the gate leading to the suburbs, we found a crowd of people, men, women, and children, streaming out toward the place where looting was going on, as if it were a fair. They were all in a very good humor, and some of the housewives were carrying baskets as they do on a market day. They moved politely aside to let us pass, not knowing who we were, and then fell into step, and marched on behind us. Among them was a man I knew, Perruche, the barber. He was carrying a paper lantern in his hand, and as I came near, he held it up to my face, and as soon as he saw who it was he called out, "Hullo, Colas! Glad to see you back! Come and have a drink."

"Tomorrow if you like," said I. "There is a time for everything."

"You must be breaking up, Breugnon. Thirst is always in season, and if we wait till tomorrow all the good wine may be gone. Is it possible that you have actually lost your taste for a good September vintage?"

"Stolen drink has no flavor."

"Stolen? You mean saved out of a burning house. I should be a pretty fool to let it all run away into the gutter."

"Thief!" said I, and pushed him out of my way, and as each man behind came up, he too said, "Thief," and frowned at the barber, who stood completely dumfounded for a moment. Then we heard him shouting, and as I looked over my shoulder I saw that he was running after us, shaking his fist. But as nobody took any more notice of him, he fell silent when he had caught up to us, and marched on behind.

The crowd was so dense when we came to the waterside, just by the first Yonne bridge, that I halted and ordered the drum to beat; this made them open a little, so that we pushed forward like a wedge; but after a few yards we could go no further. I found myself rubbing elbows with two boatmen whom I knew well; one Father Joachim, nicknamed "Calabre," and the other a man named Gadin, called Gueurlu.

"What are you doing here, Master Breugnon," said one, "all harnessed up like a prize donkey? Are you out for fun or a fight?"

"There's many a true word spoken in jest, Calabre. I have just been appointed Captain of Clamecy, and I am here to defend the town against all its enemies."

"There are no enemies that I know of," said he. "You must be cracked."

"What do you call that crowd down there, setting fire to houses?"

"We are all sorry that your house was burnt the first day, Master," said he, "but now that it is gone, I don't see what difference it makes to you if we do go for a fat old thief like Poullard, who grows rich on the wool that he pulls off our backs, and then turns up his nose at us. It is a good deed to rob the likes of him, and anyhow you are in the same boat with us poor men now, all to gain and nothing to lose, so get out of our way!"

I hated to get my hands on these poor devils, so I tried to make them hear reason first.

"You have everything to lose, Calabre," I said; "your honor to begin with."

"Honor!" cried he. "Is it good to eat? What's the use of talking about a thing like that, when you know we may soon be all dead men; dead and blown away as if we had never existed?"

"Honor, indeed!" said Gueurlu; "that's a word they put on rich men's tombstones, but when *we* die, they shovel us into the common ditch. Can you tell by the smell if we had honor or not?"

"Joachim," said I, turning away from Gueurlu, "it is true a man does not amount to much all by himself, but get a lot of men together and it's a different story; many a little makes a mickle, you know, and when the rich are all swept away and forgotten, with their lying epitaphs, down to the very names they are so proud of, then the hardworking people of Clamecy will be known as her real nobility. We must not have it said that we too were rascals."

"Much I care!" said Gueurlu, but Calabre cried, "You are a pig-face! You care for nothing, but I am like Breugnon,—I do care what they say of me, and by St. Nicholas! the rich shall not have all the honor to themselves; high or low, there is not one of them worth our little fingers!"

This brought on a great dispute. Gueurlu persisted that our betters from the least to the greatest, from our own Duke up to the princes, did nothing but grab, and stuff their bellies with other folks' dinners; and even laid hands on the King's treasures as soon as the breath was out of his body;—that there was no use in talking about "honor" after that;—we might as well take a leaf out of their book.

Calabre said they were indeed a set of hogs, and that some day our

Henry would come back from the tomb to make them disgorge, or else we would all rise ourselves, and cut their throats for them. But meanwhile, we were going to show them that there was more real honor in us than in the heart of what they call a nobleman.

"Hooray!" cried I; "you are with us then?"

"Yes, by the Mother of God! And Gueurlu is coming too."

"No, he isn't!"

"I tell you he is, or I'll pitch him neck and crop into the river! Here we go, forward march! Out of my road, wrigglers!"

He forced his way through the press, and we followed like a school of herrings. Most of the men we came up against now were so far gone in drink that there was no use in saying a word to them; anyhow, there is a time for everything, and we had got past the talking stage; there was nothing left to us but our fists; so as drunken men are safe all the world over, we just sat them down on the stones as gently as we could and went on.

By this time we had reached the warehouse gates, and could see the looters swarming all over Master Pierre Poullard's house like ants. Some were ripping open chests and bales, bedizening themselves in stolen finery; others, with shrieks of laughter, were throwing everything breakable they could find out of the windows. The courtyard was full of wine barrels and frantic drinkers. I saw one man with his mouth to the bunghole, who having drunk till he could hold no more, rolled over on his back, the red stream still spattering in his face, and running away into little pools on the ground, where children were lapping up the wine, and mud with it.

The rioters had heaped up a great pile of furniture in a corner of the court, and had set it on fire so that they might see the better. But the whole infernal orgy centered in the cellars, where from all directions came the sound of mallets, as great barrels and tuns were staved in, and the wine poured out in floods. Groans, screams, and choking coughs echoed from the low arches, as if a herd of swine had been let loose there, and already long tongues of flame and smoke came licking out of the bars of the windows. They were all so busy, each man intent on what he was doing, that no one seemed to see us as we made our way into the yard. I signed to Bardet,—he beat a long roll on his drum, and then in a voice of thunder announced my appointment as Captain. The instant he ceased I took up the word, and ordered the mob to disperse on pain of severe penalties.

At the first tap of the drum they had all drawn together like a swarm of bees, buzzing angrily; then shrieking, and hurling stones, they rushed upon us. After a fierce struggle we pushed them back, and succeeded in forcing the doors of the cellar under a hail of tiles and billets of wood from the upper windows, in spite of which we made our entrance good, and then had time to breathe and count our wounded.

Poor old Gangnot had lost another finger, and Calabre's right eye was badly injured; for me, I had caught my thumb in the hinge of the door-flap, as I banged it shut; and by my faith, it turned me sick and faint like a woman. Fortunately there was an open keg of brandy close at hand, and after I had swallowed a dram and bathed my thumb in some of the same, my head ceased to go round; but as the fight went on, the pain made me as mad as a tiger.

By this time we were inside, and all struggling together on the stairs leading from the house to the cellar, and I felt that we could not keep this up long, as these devils were discharging their muskets, close into our very faces, so that they set Saulsoy's beard on fire, and Gueurlu had to squeeze it out between his hard hands. Luckily the rioters were too drunk to shoot straight, or we none of us would have come out of it alive. I could see also that we had an ally in the fire, which was creeping round the court from wing to wing, toward the main building where we were; so when we had retreated to the topmost step, some of us stood firm, while the rest hastily raised a barrier of loose stones and rubbish, reaching to the lintel of the doorway. Through the chinks we stuck our pikes and lances, like the quills of a porcupine. "Now," cried I, "those who like fire, will soon have plenty of it!"

The cellars were full of men, for the most part too drunk to realize their danger; but when the flames appeared through the cracks of the walls and began to eat away the beams of the roof, it was a perfect pandemonium of yells and curses, and like bubbling wine in a vat they rose to the surface, and made a rush for our staircase. Some of the foremost, with their clothes actually on fire, were crushed against our barricade by the weight of those behind them, and their bodies filled the doorway from side to side, like a cork in a bottle. It was horrible to see; and also to hear the fire raging and roaring! If I had been just then the simple Breugnon of everyday life, I should have tried to save the poor screaming wretches, but when a man is in authority, he must think of nothing outside of his duty; compassion at that crisis would have been sheer weakness. I knew that the safety of the city hung on the defeat of these brigands, for if they had escaped they would have outnumbered our small forces, and with the fear of the gallows before their eyes, would have fought to desperation. No, there was now nothing for it but to smoke the wasps out of their nest.

Just at this moment whom should I see over the heads of the crowd but my old schoolfellow, Gambi! He was a good-for-nothing soaker, it is true, and had no business to be where he was, but we had been playmates from childhood, had been confirmed on the same day together, and I could not bear to leave an old chum to such a fate.

I crawled between our pikes over the barrier, and somehow forced apart the tightly wedged mass of human beings, though it seemed as if there was not room to move more than your eyelids. Gambi was tottering on the edge of the lowest step, held up by those around him, and I reached him literally walking on the bodies of the others, who snapped and tore at me in passing, so that I thought that I should have to bring him away in pieces. But there is a special Providence for drunkards,—for some of them at least,—and at last I was able to seize him by the collar, and fighting and kicking out right and left, I dragged him to the floor where the air was clearer.

There was little time to spare! The fire was roaring through the doorway, as if up a chimney, driving out men from the rampart we had made, and I could smell the roasting flesh of the brigands on the staircase. Stooping low and treading on I knew not what, I dragged Gambi by his hair through a hole in the wall, and somehow managed to reach the outside of the warehouse, leaving the fire to finish the work of destruction. When my men rejoined me they were so glad to see me safe that they could not do enough for Gambi; and after we had revived and fed him, we found under his rags some beautiful colored enamels, which he had stolen, God knows where! and contrived to hold on to during all the struggle. He was of course completely sobered by this time, and weeping with gratitude he pulled out his ill-gotten treasures, and threw them away with all his strength, declaring that stolen goods would never prosper and that he could not bear to keep them!

At sunrise the next morning Robinet appeared, triumphantly leading the Procurator, a force of thirty men at arms, and a large party of peasants. Later came the Magistrate with more reinforcements, and the next day our good Duke sent in some of his own followers. Order being now restored, they set to work. First they raked among the hot cinders, then they drew up a list of property destroyed, added their own pay and expenses, and returned whence they came,—except, of course, our own officials, who remained with us.

What then was the moral of all this experience? It is this,—help yourself, and others will help you.

XI
A Practical Joke

September 30th.

ORDER being re-established, and the ashes cooled, we heard no more talk of the plague and the riots, but for all that the city seemed crushed, and its inhabitants, still hardly recovered from their fright, appeared to feel their way; as if they did not know who was to have the upper hand in future.

For the most part men kept indoors, but if obliged to go out, they crept close along by the house walls, like a dog with his tail between his legs. The truth is, few had reason to be proud of their part in the late troubles, and a man hardly liked to look at his own face in the glass, for there he saw human nature, stripped of all disguises: — not a pretty sight, and one that makes most of us feel shamefaced and suspicious.

I too was uneasy and sad, but for different reasons: first, I was haunted by the thought of the massacre in the burning cellars; and on the other hand, when I looked in the familiar faces of my neighbors, I could not help remembering their cruelty and cowardice: this made bad feeling between us, for they knew, of course, how I felt. I longed to wipe it all out, and behave as if nothing had happened, but as that could not be, we all went about in the altered town, under the heat and languor of late summer.

Racquin had been sent to Nevers for trial; but it was a question whether he fell under the jurisdiction of the Duke or the King, so he stood a fair chance of getting off scot free. Our county authorities were kind enough to overlook my illegal conduct; — for it seems that in saving Clamecy that night, I had committed half a dozen crimes, any one of which would have been enough to bring me to the galleys; — but as none of this could have happened if they themselves had remained at the post of duty, they decided to pass it over in silence; a decision in which I naturally acquiesced. The less I have to do with courts of justice the better, I always think; for you never know how a trial will turn out, and innocence itself is no real protection. If you once get your little finger into the cursed machinery of the law, you are like to lose the whole arm, and you may have to cut that off to save your body: so between their lordships and myself there was a tacit agreement that they had seen nothing out of the way while I was Captain of Clamecy: because everything on that fateful night had been accomplished by themselves alone.

It is much easier, however, to shut one's eyes to the past than to rub it off the slate: there is such a thing as memory, and, when we met face to face, it was awkward for both parties. I could see that they had a lurking dread of me, and to tell the truth I was rather afraid myself of this absurd unknown Breugnon, who had suddenly sprung up and performed such exploits. I had never supposed myself to be an Attila or a Cæsar; my eloquence had hitherto been inspired by wine rather than by war;—and in short on both sides we were shamefaced and out of sorts in mind and body. There is no remedy like hard work, and as the riots had provided plenty to do for every one in the town, we all went at it with the utmost energy. The ruins had to be cleared away first; then by good luck the harvest that year was unusually abundant, both in grain and fruit; and as for the vintage, the oldest inhabitant could remember nothing to equal it.

Our good Mother Earth seemed to have drunk so much of our blood, only that she might restore it to us in generous wine: for nothing in this world is really wasted or lost; everything has to go somewhere. If the rain falls from the clouds and is drawn up to them again, then why should not the blood in our veins go and come between us and the earth? I have always loved to think that in some former existence I was a vigorous vine-root, and shall be one again perhaps, during a delightful immortality. How good it would be to grow and flourish, to feel my dark velvety bunches of grapes swell and fill with sweet juices, under the warm sunshine: and it must be best of all to be eaten! Setting such speculations aside, the earth bled at every pore during this wonderful season, so that we did not know what to do with the juice of our vines. As there were not casks enough to go round, masses of grapes were heaped up in vats, without even pressing them. Father Coullemard, an old man who lived at Andries, could not dispose of his crop, and so offered his grapes at the vineyard, for thirty sous a barrel.

Imagine our feelings! In our part of the world we cannot bear to throw anything away; so, as there was nothing for it but to drink the wine on the spot, we all did our duty like men. The labors of Hercules were nothing to it, but I am afraid that the hero himself, and not Antæus, fell and touched Mother Earth!

Everybody felt cheerful and more like himself when this was over, but still there was something unpleasant,—a sort of constraint among us, and even in the midst of our carouses there was altogether too much solitary drinking,—in my opinion an evil and unhealthy practice. How long this sort of thing would have lasted, I cannot undertake to say, but chance intervened, and once more brought us all together. Love can unite *two* hearts, but the only thing that can make a large number of men act as one, is the fear of a common enemy; and in our case, this enemy was our master. Duke Charles of Nevers took it into his head this year to forbid our games and dances, and as a natural consequence, every one who was not crippled with gout, and who could put foot to the ground, was seized with a perfect passion for dancing.

No one exactly understood why, but the bone of contention between the Duke and the town had always been the Count's Meadows, which lie outside the gates, at the foot of Picon Hill, watered by the Beuvron, which winds through them like a silver serpent. For more years than any one can remember, there had been a dispute about these meadows: pull devil, pull baker, and it was a question which had got the best of it. Of course the contest was conducted with the utmost politeness on both sides;—"My friends of the good town of Clamecy," and "Your Lordship's most obedient";—but neither party would yield an inch, for all that.

When we had resort to the courts, we always got the worst of it; the judgment rendered being invariably that our meadows did not belong to us; but this did not bother us in the least, as we had reason to know that justice can make black seem white—at a price.

Possession, however, is nine points of the law, so we just held on to our playground, which had special advantages, because it was the only bit of land which was not the private property of some one in the town, and therefore might be said to belong to us all; or perhaps to the Duke, which came to much the same thing. Being common property, we did not mind spoiling it, and anything that was not convenient to do on our own premises, we did on the Count's Meadows. We washed clothes, carded wool, and beat carpets; there was a large rubbish heap there, and many goats led out to pasture. On fine days we played games, or danced to a hurdy-gurdy; we shot at a target, and practised the drum and trumpet, and at night there were any number of loving couples along the banks of the Beuvron, which took it all as a matter of course, though he saw enough to frighten most rivers.

All went well as long as our old Duke Louis lived, for he shut his eyes to our goings on, being a man of sense who knew that you must not keep too tight a hand on the reins; he let us prance about and play the fool a little, knowing all the while that he was the master. His son, on the contrary, has the kind of conceit that prefers the show of power to the reality, and likes to mount his high horse on slight provocation. He ought to have known that a Frenchman will always sing and make fun of his rulers, and if that is not allowed, he rebels; for he cannot bear people who insist on being taken seriously, and loves those he can laugh at, or with, for laughter puts all men on a level.

The Duke, then, issued an order forbidding us to play, dance, dig, walk on the grass, or trespass in any way on the Count's Meadows: and a good time he chose for this piece of foolishness, just after all our misfortunes, when instead of annoying us, he ought at the very least to have remitted some of our taxes. He soon found, however, that the Clamecyans are not made of soft fiber, but are tough as old oaks, so that if you drive in a wedge you have hard work to get it out again. There was no need to call a meeting to protest against the edict; from all sides arose a deafening clamor: — "What, take away our meadows? The ground that he had given us! (or that we had taken, it is all the same!) — land that we stole four hundred years ago, which has been doubly sacred to us ever since? — all the dearer that we have been obliged to struggle for it day by day, and inch by inch; holding on to it by sheer tenacity! It was enough to discourage a man from ever taking what did not belong to him; enough really to make him sick of living! Our dead would turn in their graves if we were weak enough to yield on a point thus involving the honor of the city. The fatal order was proclaimed with beat of drum, by the town crier, who looked as if he were going to execution; and that very evening, there was a meeting held of all the men of importance in the city; the heads of guilds, the chiefs of brotherhoods and corporations, and those who represented the various districts, came together under the arches of the market. I was there, for St. Anne's, and, as you may suppose, there were different opinions among the delegates as to what ought to be done.

Gangnot, in the name of St. Eloi, and Calabre, for St. Nicholas, advocated strong measures; they wanted to set fire to the fences round the fields, break down the gates, knock the sergeants on the head, and rip up the meadows from end to end. On the other side, were Florimond, the baker, for St. Honoré, and Maclou, the gardener, for St. Fiacre; they advised a more diplomatic course, a war of words, and parchments, a petition to the Duchess, accompanied, perhaps, by some cakes and some garden stuff. Fortunately three of us, Jean Bobin for St. Crispin, Émond Poifu for St. Vincent, and I, were not disposed either to grovel before the Duke, or to kick his head off. Keep in the middle of the road, was our motto. In our part of the world we like to get the better of people without too much fuss and expense: it is all very well to revenge yourself, but why not have a little fun out of it at the same time? We hit at last upon a splendid idea — but I am not going to tell you now what it was, for that would spoil the joke. I will only say to the credit of all of us, that for a whole fortnight the great secret was kept perfectly, though it was known to the entire town. The honor of first having thought of it belongs to me, but they all added something, here a touch and there another, till there was nothing lacking. The Mayor and Aldermen kept themselves informed of our progress, in the discreetest manner; and Master Delavau, the notary, would come slinking in every evening with his cloak drawn up around his face, to show us how to creep through the meshes of the law, while appearing to respect it; and would draw up long Latin addresses to the Duke, expressed in the most submissive terms on the part of his contumacious vassals. When the great day arrived, the town guilds and companies with their masters assembled at St. Martin's Place, all dressed in their best, and drawn up around their banners.

As ten strokes sounded from the great tower, the bells began to ring, and on both sides of the square the doors of St. Martin's and of the Town Hall were thrown open. From the church issued the long procession of white-robed clergy, and on the steps of the Town Hall appeared the green and yellow gowns of the Mayor and aldermen. These dignified bodies exchanged profound bows over the heads of us, who stood below them; and then they marched slowly down; first the beadles, with their red cloaks and redder noses, and then the town bailiffs, adorned with their gold chains of office, and striking their staves loudly on the pavement as they advanced.

We formed a great ring around the square, with our backs to the houses; and the authorities placed themselves just in the middle.

The whole town was there to the last man; the pettifoggers and barristers were ranged under the banner of St. Ives, (the man of business of Our Father,) while the apothecaries, leeches and mediciners, men of St. Cosmo, formed a guard of honor around the Mayor and the old Archdeacon. The only absentee was the Procurator: he was indeed the Duke's representative, but he had married an alderman's daughter, and his interests being thus divided, he did not want to be forced to take part with one side or the other, and so found means to keep out of the way.

We all waited there for a little while; the square seething with noise and laughter, like a vat in ferment. Every one talked at once, fiddles squeaked, and dogs barked: what were we waiting for? Something is coming, a surprise! and before we could see anything we heard shouts drawing nearer, and all heads turned at once, like weathercocks when the wind changes. A procession now advanced from the end of Market Street, and at its head, borne on the shoulders of eight stout porters, was a pyramid-shaped structure, looking like three tables placed one above the other. The legs were all wreathed with bright silks and flowers, and from the highest hung long streamers of colored ribbon, cords and tassels; on the top was an ornamented dais supporting a veiled statue.

As we were all in the secret, no one expressed surprise, and though bursting with laughter, we took off our hats and bowed deeply. When the platform reached the center of the square, it made a stop between the Mayor and the vicar, and then all the corporations and districts, each preceded by its players, made one turn about the square, and wheeling round the corner of the church, entered the little street which goes down to the Beuvron gate. St. Nicholas came first, as of right, with Calabre leading, strutting along dressed in a church cope, and glittering like a beetle with gold embroidery. He carried the device of the river saint, a boat in which were three little children, and was escorted by four boatmen, bearing enormous yellow candles as big as a man's leg, and as hard as bricks; ready for any emergency. Then came St. Eloi, with his copper-workers, locksmiths and blacksmiths; poor Gangnot, with the fingers that were left to him, holding a cross engraved with the badge of a hammer and anvil. Next, barrel-makers, vintagers, and vinegrow-ers marched after their St. Vincent, with a jug in one hand, and a bunch of grapes in the other. St. Joseph and St. Anne followed, mother and son-in-law, with the carpenters and wood-carvers, and then St. Honoré, covered with flour. He bore a sort of Roman trophy in his hand, like a lance thrust through a round loaf with a crown above it. After him were the cobblers and leather-dressers, under St. Crispin;—last and best of all, came the gardeners, men and women, carrying carnations and roses, their spades and rakes all twined with flowers; their fine red silk banner streaming in the wind showed St. Fiacre, bare-legged, dig-ging up the ground.

After all these, the veiled platform moved on majestically. Before it went girls in white, chanting and scattering flowers: the Mayor and his staff marched solemnly on either side, holding the ends of the long streamers which hung from the dais, while the guilds of St. Ives and St. Cosmo formed an imposing escort. Then came the verger of St. Mar-tin's, strutting like a game-cock, preceding two priests, one long and thin, the other short and fat; and the vicar himself, his hands folded over his portly stomach, singing litanies in his deep bass voice as he walked; or rather giving out a booming note from time to time, while the others did the work.

The general public brought up the rear in a miscellaneous mass, like a flood held back, as it were, by our procession. In this order we ad-vanced through the city gate, straight towards the Count's Meadows, in the midst of a whirl of golden plane leaves, stripped from the trees by the wind and sent fluttering before us into the sluggish river, on which they drifted like flakes of gold. At the entrance to the Meadows there was a guard of three policemen and a Captain, in command at the château. The latter was a new broom, and being eager to magnify his office, he rolled his eyes and frowned severely at us; but his own men and the citizens understood one another, and they only opposed us for form's sake. We, on our side, made believe to be offended, and demanded a passage with much noise and profanity, but we had hard work to keep our faces straight, and besides it would have been risky to go on in this way much longer, for Calabre and his men, getting out of hand, began to brandish their big candles about the ears of the police. So the Mayor stepped forward, raised his cap at arm's length from his head, and cried: "Hats off!" At the word, the veil which hid the statue fell to the ground, and the town bailiffs with loud voices proclaimed: "Place for his Lordship the Duke!" Instantly the tumult ceased, the saints and their followers ranged themselves on both sides of the way, and respectfully presented arms; while the Captain and his satellites, hastily pulling off their hats, stood aside to make way for the platform, on which was perched the Duke in effigy. He wobbled slightly, as his porters bore him along, but by the plumed hat, sword, and wreath of laurels, it was easy to recognize him; and to put the matter beyond doubt, there was a pompous Latin inscription at the base of the dais, proclaiming his dignity to all the world.

The features were perhaps not a perfect likeness, but as we had not had the time to make a new statue we had just taken an old wooden figure, which we found stuck away in the garret of the Town Hall. We did not know who or what it represented, but on the pedestal was the half-effaced name of Balthazar, which we afterward shortened to Balduke. No one cared whether the statue resembled the Duke or not; statues seldom do look like the people that they are supposed to represent; witness those of the saints, or our Lord Himself; but to the eye of faith they are perfectly satisfactory, and as a devout believer sees his god in a log of wood, just so that day we saw our Duke before us.

All obstacles being removed, his Lordship proudly entered his own meadows, and we naturally followed; banners waving, drums beating, trumpets sounding, and the Holy Sacrament as a fitting climax. No loyal subject would have dared to offer any objection, so even the sulky Captain was obliged to choose between stopping the Duke or following him, and he decided to fall into step with us. And now, with victory in sight, we very nearly came to grief at the eleventh hour; for a dispute arose as to who should pass in first, and all considerations due to age or sex were completely forgotten. St. Eloi and St. Nicholas jostled one another, St. Joseph was rude to his mother-in-law, and as we were all somewhat over-excited, the consequences might have been serious. Fortunately I was able to intervene with success, having a foot in every camp. My name is Nicholas, my trade is under the protection of Sts. Joseph and Anne, and the patron of vineyards, St. Vincent, may be called my foster brother, as he and I have sucked at the same breast; so I belong to all the saints, if only they are on my side.

Just then I happened to spy a country cart passing, and who should be lurching along beside it but my friend Gambi? "Comrades!" I cried, "we must not try to get ahead of each other on this glorious day; the greatest among us is here;—after the Duke, of course! so give three cheers for Bacchus!" Whereupon I caught Gambi by the slack of his breeches and threw him up into the cart, where he alighted in a cask of grapes; then seizing the reins, we drove in triumphantly; first Bacchus sitting in his cask, kicking his legs and laughing fit to kill himself; and then all the procession following arm in arm, dancing with joy. It was delightful to be once more in our dear Meadows; and there we stayed all day, and far into the night, cooking, eating, and playing around the statue of the good Duke.

The place looked like a pigsty the next day; there was not a single blade of grass left, and the print of our feet was stamped deep all over the ground, as a proof of the devotion with which his loyal subjects had feasted their suzerain. He must have been hard to please if he was not satisfied, and we on our part were delighted with the events of the day.

An inquiry was indeed started by the Procurator, who professed to be indignant, and threatened us with dire consequences; but on second thoughts he found it wiser to let the whole thing drop; since no one really wanted to close the door so happily reopened.

This was the method we chose to show that we could be true subjects of the Duke and King, and yet insist on having our own way — for there is no denying that we are a stiff-necked generation — and this being done, the town seemed to pick up its spirits after the trials it had passed through, and we were once more all good friends together.

We would wink and slap each other on the back, when we met, and say that people had better let us alone, as the good tricks were not yet all out of the bag; and so in this way the memory of our misfortunes died away and was forgotten.

XII
Other People's Houses

October.

After much delay I was finally obliged to settle down somewhere; I kept putting it off on the pretense that I wanted to look carefully over the ground, but I had to come to it at last, much against my will. At first the whole town was open to me, and my friends were eager to offer me a bed for a night or two; every one naturally pitied a man whose hearth was a heap of cold cinders, and wanted to give him what help they could; "at first" I say, but as the recollection of our disasters faded away, people began once more to draw back into their shells, — except poor victims like me who had no shells left to draw into.

My children would have been shocked at the bare idea of my living at the inn; such a thing was never heard of among good Clamecyans of our sort, and, though it was not exactly a matter of feeling with my sons, there was the terrible question to be considered — "What would people say?" There was no hurry, of course, on their part or on mine; we both tried to put off the evil day, for I am altogether too outspoken to be at my ease in bigoted households such as theirs, so we dodged around the question in a most uncomfortable state of mutual embarrassment.

Martine got us out of our dilemma by insisting that I must come to her, for she really does love and want me; — but there was my son-in-law. Naturally there was no reason why he should wish to have me as a permanent member of his household, and so there we all were! This made me feel as if my poor old bones were being put up for sale, and I kept out of their way as much as possible, while on their side they watched me with a suspicious eye.

I took refuge for a short time on the slopes of Beaumont in that little hut where I had been so sick with the plague in July; for the joke of it was that though the mob had burned my healthy house they left standing the worthless shed where Death and I had slept together, and now that he had no more terrors for me it was really a pleasure to go back to the poor little place with its trampled floor, still littered with the empty bottles of my somewhat funereal orgy.

The place was uninhabitable in winter, as I knew well enough; the door was half off its hinges, the window panes cracked, and the roof leaked like a sieve; but tomorrow can take care of the things of itself, and today, at least, there was no prospect of rain, so I put off all thought of the future till the week after next. "It will be time enough to cross the bridge when I come to it," thought I, "and perhaps the world will come to an end between now and then. I should be vexed enough if I heard the Angel Gabriel blowing his horn just after I had swallowed such a bitter pill; no, I like to drink my pleasure fresh out of the barrel, but disagreeable things can always stand till they get stale."

Well, there I waited, holding my troubles at arm's length, but I did not give myself up exclusively to meditation. Behind my locked gates, I dug in my garden, covered up all the roots snugly against the winter, raked away the fallen leaves from the paths, and, generally, made the place tidy; then there was a little tree on which still hung a few red and yellow pears, and my delight was to lie on the sunny bank and let the sweet juice slip gently down my throat.

I only went to town when it was absolutely necessary to replenish my store of provisions and news, and when I was there I carefully avoided my sons, having given out that I had gone on a journey. They may not have thought this story literally true, but it would have been disrespectful to contradict a report started by their father, so we kept on playing our little game of hide-and-go-seek until Martine upset it all.

We had not taken her sufficiently into our calculations, and, like most of her sex, she had no idea of playing fair, and being besides thoroughly up to all my tricks, she found me without much trouble. She is anyhow a great stickler for duty, family feeling, and all that sort of thing. One evening when I was working in the garden, I caught sight of my daughter coming up the hill; I made one jump into the house, and, locking the door, lay down against the wall. In a minute or two I heard her steps, and then she tried the door, shook it, knocked, and called out to me; I lay there like a dead leaf, holding my breath, though I had a tickling in my throat and wanted dreadfully to cough. (I don't know why, but it always happens like that.) It was not so easy to get rid of her, however; she kept battering at the door and window, and calling, "Father, let me in! I know you are there; let me in!"

"What a minx it is!" I said to myself. "I should have no chance at all if that door gave way."

I had half a mind to open it myself and give her a good hug, but I hate to yield about anything, so I lay still and after a little while she got tired and stopped her pounding; then I could hear her walking slowly down the path. I came out of my corner and began to laugh, and cough and laugh again till I was nearly choking, and when I got over the fit, and stopped to wipe my eyes, I heard a voice behind me saying, "You ought to be ashamed of yourself!"

It nearly knocked me flat, but I turned my head and there on top of the wall was Martine looking at me.

"I've got you now, you old joker!" she cried.

"I'm caught, sure enough," said I, and we both laughed to our hearts' content.

As soon as I had let her in she stood sternly before me, then grabbed me by the beard. "Say you're sorry," she cried.

You know how it is at confession; you repent, meaning to do it again the next opportunity, so I replied meekly, "*Mea culpa!*"

But she kept pulling me to and fro, declaring that it was a disgrace for an old white-beard like me to have no more sense than a baby; finally she gave me a last pull and tap on the cheek, and threw her arms round my neck saying, "Why didn't you come to me, Father, when you know how much I want you?"

"My dear little girl, I will explain all about it."

"You can explain as we go along, you are coming home with me this minute."

"Martine, you must give me time to pack up my things."

"I'll do your packing," cried she, and with that she threw an old cloak over my shoulders, jammed my hat on my head, picked up my bundle, and told me to come along. I sat down on the step and said there was no hurry, which made her furiously angry.

"Why do you object to coming to my house?" said she.

"I don't object, I know sooner or later I shall have to do it."

"That's a pretty way to talk," said she. "I don't believe you care anything about me!"

"You know very well how much I love you, darling! but you are dearer to me in my own house, than in an outsider's!"

"Do you mean to say I am an outsider?"

"You are half one, you see!"

"Nothing of the sort! I am just myself, as you know perfectly well; his wife, of course, just as he is my husband, and I go his way as long as he goes mine, but you can set your mind at rest, he will be perfectly charmed to have you in the house, or else I will know the reason why!"

"I've had plenty of lodgers of that sort," said I, "when our Lord of Nevers billeted them on us, but I had rather not be one my own self."

"You will have to learn," said she. "Come, I am waiting."

"Agreed; but on condition that you will take me in on my own terms."

"You are a perfect old tyrant! but there, I promise!"

"On your honor?"

"Yes, yes, now that's enough talking, I won't wait another minute," and she seized my arm in such a grip that I had to go willy-nilly.

When we got to her house, she showed me with pride the room she had arranged for me behind the shop, all warm and comfortable and directly under her eye, as if I were a child of a year old. I was touched to see how the dear girl had made up the bed with her best linen sheets and comforter, and had put a nosegay on the table; it made me laugh too when I thought how furious she would be. "This won't do at all," said I, so though vexed enough she showed me the other rooms downstairs, but I would have none of them, and finally chose a little nook under the mansarded roof.

In spite of everything she could say, I declared that she might take it or leave it, that if she would not let me have the room I liked, I would go back to my hut, so she had to give in, but every day and all day long she kept at me about it.

"That's not a fit place for you, Father, the other room is much more comfortable,—why in the world don't you like it?"

"Because I don't," I would say and then she would go into a rage, and swear that I would drive her crazy, that she knew why I behaved so, it was just because I was too stuffy and proud to be beholden to any of my children, even to her.

"I should like to box your ears!" she would cry, and then I would tell her that would be the only way to make me accept something from her gratis.

"You don't love me, Daddy."

"Now, my little girl, my own sweet baby!"

"Let me alone! Don't you dare to touch me! You can't make up to me like that, old fraud that you are! And all the time you are just laughing at me. I can see your mouth twitching."

"You're laughing yourself, Martine," and I put my finger on her cheek, which broke into a smile.

"All the same, I am really angry," said she, "even if you do make me laugh with your nonsense, but in my heart I think you are a horrid old thing! You have lost your house and you are too stuck-up to let your daughter help you; it is nothing but wicked pride, and you have no right to behave so!"

"It is the only right that is left to me," said I.

But that did not end the matter and there was never any lack of sharp words between two people like us, who both of us had a fine edge to our tongues; but, luckily, a joke could always make us laugh in the midst of our discussions and so the storm would blow over.

One evening when her tongue had been going like a clapper, and I had long ceased to listen, I told her at last it was time to stop, and wait for the rest till the next day.

"Very well then," she said. "Good-night! But won't you change your mind, old Peacock?"

"Listen, dear, I am proud as a peacock, if you choose to say so, but, frankly now, in my place what would you do?"

"Pretty much the same thing."

"Well, then, you see! Now give me a kiss for good-night."

She did kiss me but I could hear her muttering to herself that it was hard luck for her to have two such wooden heads in one family.

"Well, pound the other one as much as you please, but leave me in peace."

"He will get his share, never fear, and you too," she answered; and then the next day it began all over again, so that I really thought on the whole I had more than was due to me.

For the first few days I was in clover, and every one petted and spoiled me; even Florimond, who overwhelmed me with attentions greater than I desired or deserved, for I saw that Martine was keeping her eye on him. Glodie was always twittering around me; I had the most comfortable chair; I was helped first at table, and when I spoke every one listened in respectful silence. It was all perfectly delightful, but I felt that I could not stand much more; it made me restless, and I kept going up and down stairs all day long to and from my garret. This, naturally, got on everybody's nerves, and Martine, who is by no means the most patient of women, was nearly beside herself when she heard the stairs creak for the hundredth time under my feet. If it had been summer, I should have gone out and roamed about the country, but as it was I had to do my roaming indoors. It was a cold early autumn, the fields were damp and misty, and it rained from morning till night; so I was shut up in the house, and not my house, Heaven help me!

I hated all the furniture and ornaments, for Florimond's taste in such things is stupid and pretentious, and it made me so uncomfortable that my fingers fairly itched to move things round, or alter them, but of course, that would never do with the master of the house standing by, and the slightest criticism was a mortal offense. In the dining-room there was a ewer decorated with a simpering lady, her tiresome lover and two cooing doves which made me ill whenever I looked at it. I told Florimond it made the victuals stick in my throat, and begged him to take it away at mealtimes; but his notion of art was ornamented confectionery and he greatly admired this piece, so he refused, as, of course, he had a perfect right to do; but the faces I made amused the whole household.

What was to be done? Laugh at me for an old fool? By all means; but at night, in my garret, when the rain was on the roof, I turned and twisted in my bed, not daring to shake the house by walking up and down with my heavy tread. One night as I sat up there, bare-legged, meditating on these things, a thought came into my head that sooner or later, by hook or by crook, I must rebuild my house, and after that I felt happier; but I kept my little plan to myself and did not breathe a word of it to my children, for I knew what they would say.

"Where was the money to come from?"

Alas! we are no longer in the times of Orpheus and Amphion, when stones built themselves into walls as if to the sound of music; there is no such charm to raise them now unless it be the chink of money bags, and that was always faint with me and now completely inaudible.

I resolved to have recourse to my friend Paillard, though, if the truth were told, he had never offered to lend me money; but since I took a sincere pleasure in asking him, why should he not find equal delight in giving me what I needed?

Arguing in this way, I took advantage of a comparatively fine day and went to Dornecy. Everything spoke of sadness; the dark hovering clouds, the muddy ground, the damp gusts of wind swooping like the wings of a great bird, tearing the yellow leaves from the trees and scattering them over the fields.

Paillard could hardly wait to let me get out my first sentence before he interrupted me to complain of the hard times, the falling off of his business, the bad debts he had, lack of money, et cetera, till I pulled him up short by asking him if he would like me to lend him a penny piece?

It would be hard to say which of us was the more irritated and hurt by this little passage at arms, but we kept up the conversation for a while longer, talking in a stiff unnatural way of the weather and the crops. I could see that he was sorry for his meanness; the poor old boy is good-hearted at bottom and genuinely attached to me, and I knew that he would have been delighted to lend me money, if he had been certain that he would lose nothing by it, and what is more he would have yielded if I had pressed the point; but he was not to blame, after all; he had centuries of miserly blood in his veins, and though there may be small householders in his position who are also open-handed,—I say there is a legend that such people do exist,—when you lay a finger on the purse of a man like that, his first instinct is to say "No!"

At that very moment Paillard would have loved to reconsider his refusal, but here my pride came in, and I would make no further advances; my friend ought to have been glad to help me out of my difficulties, and if he thought otherwise, so much the worse for him!

There we sat sulky and unhappy; he asked if I would not stay to lunch, but I refused somewhat curtly, though I could see it nearly broke his heart, and he followed me to the door with a hang-dog expression; but as my foot was on the threshold, something came over me; I put my arm around his old neck and embraced him; he did the same to me, and there we stood without a word for a minute or two.

At last he said timidly, "Colas, I could let you have a little."

"Say no more about it," I answered, for I am an obstinate devil.

"Well," he said, "you will at least stay to luncheon?"

So we sat down and ate heartily enough, but nothing would have induced me to borrow of him now; I am made like that, and if I suffered for it this time, why so of course did he.

The question for me now was how to rebuild my house without money or workmen,—but when I get an idea in my head!

I ruminated over it as I walked back to Clamecy, and the first thing I did was to go over the ruins of my house, carefully sorting out everything that might be of use, from the half-burnt beams to the rusty hinges and black tottering walls.

One day I stole off to Chevroches to see what I could find in the quarries among the great stone blocks like the bones of our earth with their red veins. On my way through the forest, I am afraid I helped some old oaks to sink into their final repose; an illegal act perhaps, but one would not get far in this world if one only did what the law allows. The wood belonged to the town, and therefore to me, in part at least, and of course I should not have dreamed of taking more than my just share; but the thing was, how to get it home? And here the neighbors came to my assistance. One lent me his cart, another his oxen, and a third his tools, or rather his hands, which cost nothing. A man will lend anything in these parts, except his wife or his money, and I feel that way myself, for money means the future; it is hope, all that we have, the rest is only the present, which scarcely belongs to us.

At last Robinet and I began to put up the first scaffolding, but by that time it was cold weather, and every one thought I was out of my mind. I was urged to wait at least until spring, while my children made such a pother that my life was a burden to me.

In spite of all this I persisted in going on with my work, partly because I like to rub people up the wrong way, and then, though of course I knew that I could not build a house all by myself in the depths of winter, I really meant only to put up a mere shed, a sort of rabbit hutch, where I could live alone. I am sociable enough, but I like to choose my own time and place, and I am also a talker, but sometimes Breugnon seems to me the best companion in the world, and I would walk ten miles to get at him. It was, therefore, for the sake of enjoying my own charming society that I was obstinately bent on building, in spite of the opinion of the world and the remonstrances of my children.

Unluckily, I was not to have the last word, for, one frosty morning at the end of October, when the roofs of the town and the pavements were all covered with a thin glare of ice, I slipped on one of the rungs of my ladder and the next thing I knew I was lying on the ground.

"He has killed himself!" cried poor Binet, as he ran to pick me up.

"I did it on purpose," said I and tried to rise, but I could not stand as my ankle was broken.

They fetched a stretcher and carried me home, Martine and most of her neighbors by my side, wringing their hands and bewailing my sad fate. It was like an Entombment by an early master, with the Marys surrounding the body and making noise enough to wake Him.

I pretended to be unconscious so as to escape the flood of pity and reproaches, but though I lay still, with my head thrown back, and my beard pointing to Heaven, within me I was in a proper rage, in spite of this calm exterior.

XIII
Plutarch's Lives

October 30th.

I was much depressed by my accident, as may be imagined. If only the Lord had been pleased to break any other bone in my body, I thought, but here I was pinned by the leg! It is true that I should have grumbled somewhat if I had broken an arm or a rib; but now, I was ready to curse Him for His cruelty; (Praise be to His Holy Name!) and to swear that He had picked out the very thing that would vex me the most.

He knows well that my hard-won liberty, child not of gods, but of men, is to me as the breath of my nostrils; dearer than gold and silver, food and drink; and that is why He must laugh to Himself when He sees me lying here on my back like a beetle, staring at the beams and spider's webs of my garret ceiling. All the same, there is some fight left in me, though I am tied and trussed up here like a fowl on the spit. My body cannot stir an inch, it is true; but how about the spirit? My free fancies fly away on strong wings, with not a broken bone among them; and he had need to be swift who would catch and stop them.

For the first day or two I was in an execrable humor, and made good use of my tongue as the only weapon I had with which to hit out at every one, right and left; so that it was hardly safe to come near me. The worst of all was that in my heart I knew that my accident was entirely my own fault; and what made it harder to bear was that every one I saw dinned the same thing into my ears; telling me that a man of my age had no business to be climbing up ladders, like a fly on a wall; reminding me that I had had ample warning, and lamenting that I had such an obstinate nature that good advice was thrown away on me. The moral drawn, of course, was that I richly deserved my fate.

All this naturally was extremely consoling to me, — as if it was not bad enough to be in my miserable condition, without being told that I was a fool into the bargain. Martine and her husband, and all my friends and neighbors seemed to have agreed among themselves to harp on the same string whenever they came to see me, while I had to lie and listen to it all, like a helpless wild creature caught in a trap; until I lost all patience one day, when even my little Glodie began to sing the same tune:

"You were a naughty Grandad to climb up ladders!"

I tore my nightcap off my head and threw it at her. "Get out of this, you little beast!" I yelled; and then I was alone, and found that, after all, I did not like that much better.

After a while my daughter proposed, like the good girl that she is, to carry my mattress down into the room behind the shop; but I was just perverse enough to say no, again, because I had said it before; though by this time I was dying to give in. On the other hand, I hated to have strangers see me in such a state, and then Martine kept at me like a fly, (or a woman,) and could not understand that she talked too much about it, and so injured her own cause. I knew also that if I yielded I should never hear the last of it; so I told her to let me alone, and that is what it finally came to: they all went away and left me to myself, as I had wished; so surely I had nothing to complain of.

I had not been willing to tell my real reason, which was, that being a dependent in that house, I hated to give any more trouble than was necessary; but for a man who wanted people to love him, the stupidest thing I could have done was to drive them all away from me; for they took me at my word and soon forgot me, — "Out of sight, out of mind," — and no one came to see me any more, not even Glodie, though I could hear her laughing downstairs, and smiled at the sound of it; and then sighed, because I could not go and join in the fun as I used to do.

"Ungrateful little puss," I thought, but I knew that I should have done the same in her place, so I blew a kiss towards the stairs. "Have a good time, my pretty one!" — Job lay on his dunghill, you know, and railed at his fate, and I was somewhat in the same position by this time.

One day while I was thus agreeably occupied, old Paillard came in; he had a package in his hand, and sat down awkwardly enough, on the foot of my bed; while I received him in a rather crusty manner. He began to talk of one thing and another, but I contradicted every word he said; till at last he was completely put out of countenance, and sat there, clearing his throat, and tapping on the footboard of the bed. I begged him to stop, in an icy tone, and after that he simply did not dare to move a finger. I could hardly help laughing, and thought: "He reproaches himself because he knows that if he had lent me money, I should not have tried to build the wall, and so break my leg. If it had not been for his meanness, none of all this would have happened." And he did not know what to say, and I would not speak, we kept silence for some time, till at last I broke out, "Why don't you say something? Any one would think that I was actually at the last gasp; but there's no use in sitting staring at me like a stuck pig! If you can't talk, go home! You do not go to see sick people just to hold your tongue; and for goodness' sake stop fiddling with that book, or whatever it is you have got there!"

The poor old fellow stood up. "I am going, Colas," he said gently. "I can see that the sight of me puts you out, but I thought — I had brought you this book, — *Lives of Celebrated Men,* by Plutarch; it is translated by Jacques Amyot, Bishop of Auxerre; — would you like it? — it might amuse you. It would perhaps be some consolation or companionship!" I could see that his mind was not quite made up, for it was like drawing teeth for him to lend his books, which he cherished even more dearly than his ducats.

If any one dared touch one of the precious volumes in his library, he was like a lover who sees rude hands laid on the lady of his affections. I was touched and softened by the greatness of the sacrifice, and held out my hand to my old comrade, telling him how grateful I was for his kindness to such a brute as I had shown myself to be; and I took the book from his reluctant fingers.

"Take good care of it," said he.

"Make your mind easy, it shall lie under my pillow," and with this reassuring reply I let him depart.

Plutarch of Cheronæus was a stout little volume, as broad as it was long, of about thirteen hundred closely printed pages; the words all heaped one upon another, like corn in a bin. "There is three years' provender there, for three donkeys," thought I. At the head of each chapter were round medallion portraits of the illustrious subjects of the memoirs, surrounded by wreaths of laurel; these diverted me extremely; they only lacked a bunch of parsley in their mouths to be complete.

"What are all these Greeks and Romans to me?" I thought. "We are living, and they are long since dead, and can teach me nothing but what I knew before; that man is a wicked creature, but agreeable enough; that age improves wine, and spoils women; that in all countries, the big fishes swallow the little ones, and the weak jeer at their oppressors. — These Romans are terrible fellows to make long speeches; and I am not by any means opposed to eloquence; only I want to warn these gentlemen that turn and turn about is fair play."

Fluttering the leaves with a condescending air, I threw my eyes along the pages, as an angler draws his line along a stream, and hang me if I did not hook something at the very first cast. No one ever saw better fishing; the cork went under as soon as it touched the water; and such fish as I pulled up! Gold and silver, some with shining scales like jewels, scattering a shower of sparks around them; jumping and twisting, too, with quivering fins, and flapping tails. To think of my saying that they were dead!

From that day, the world might have come to an end without my knowing what had happened; my eye was fastened on my fishing line, waiting for a bite. What monster am I now to draw from the deep? Ha! look at this splendid fellow, with his white belly and his coat of mail, changeable green and blue, all shining in the sun. Honestly, the best part of my life, (days, weeks, or years, — I kept no count of them,) was spent then: and God be thanked! who gave us eyes, through which the wonderful visions in books can reach our brains. Give us only those closely packed little black marks, between the borders of the white page, and from their sight the magician conjures up long-dispersed armies, ruined cities, great orators of Rome, fierce enemies, heroes and the beauties that beguile them, the winds that blow, the sparkling sea, the hot eastern sun, and the snows of winter.

Here I can see imperial Caesar, pale and thin, reclining in his litter surrounded by his grim old soldiers; or that guzzler, Antony, with his dishes and cups, on his way to some green nook, where he and his parasites can stuff and swill to their hearts' content; devouring eight roasted boars at one sitting. Then Pompey passes, stiff and formal, with Flora whom he loves; — Poliorcites decked with a gold mantle, embroidered with the sun, moon and stars; and Artaxerxes, like a great bull among his herd of four hundred women.

Now comes Alexander, beautiful as the god Bacchus, whose dress he wears, returning in his triumph from India. See him high in a great car drawn by eight horses and covered with rich carpets and garlands of green leaves; hear the strains of flutes and hautboys as he feasts and drinks with his generals, all of them crowned with flowers: women leaping about him in the dance, and his great army at his back. Wasn't it marvelous? Then there was Queen Cleopatra, Lamia the flute-player, and Statira, who was so beautiful that it hurt your eyes to look at her! In spite of Antony, Alexander, and Artaxerxes, all these enchantresses are mine, now at my pleasure. I can enter their bowers, drink with Thaïs, embrace Roxana, and carry Cleopatra away in my arms wrapped in her carpet. It is possible for me even to imitate Antiochus, who was in love with his mother-in-law, although that is a singular idea to my notion.

I go out to exterminate the Gauls; I come, I see, I conquer; and the best of it all is that it does not cost me one single drop of blood! Then, too, my riches are beyond counting; each story is a caravel, laden with the treasures of the East or Barbary; bringing precious metals, old wines, strange beasts, and captured slaves of the rarest beauty: — such breasts, such ivory limbs! All this is mine, these empires rose, flourished and disappeared, only to give me pleasure. I feel as if I were at a Carnival, where in turn I can wear every man's mask and disguise, even to putting on his skin, and with it his thoughts and passions. Thus I am at once the music, and the dancer, the book and old Plutarch, who was inspired to write it in a most fortunate hour.

How good it is to let the rhythm of words and phrases carry you off, dancing and laughing, into space, free from all trammels of the body. This mind, this thought of ours is God Himself. Praise be to His Holy Spirit! — Sometimes I pause in the midst of the story to imagine how it will turn out, and then compare my own fancy with the image which nature or art had created. In the case of art, I am so sharp that I can generally guess right; and then how I laugh at my own cleverness! But the old witch, life, is often too much for me! — her resources are beyond our feeble comprehension. There is only one part of the tale which she never troubles herself to vary; all her stories end in the same way — wit, war, love — you know what happens to them — they disappear into the darkness; and on this one point she certainly does repeat herself.

She is like a naughty child, breaking her toys when she is tired of them, till I am provoked to blame her for being so destructive, and snatch the pieces out of her hands; but it is too late; they are broken past repair; and all that I can do, is to cherish what is left, as Glodie rocks the remains of her doll in her arms.

At each revolution of the dial this Death comes nearer and nearer, like a beautiful refrain: "Strike hour! ring bells, ding dong ding." Now, I fancy myself Cyrus, Emperor of Persia, Conqueror of Asia; hear what I say: — "Friend, envy me not the small space of earth, which covers my poor body." — I stand beside Alexander as he reads this epitaph and trembles, for in it he seems to hear his own voice rising from the tomb.

Now that you are dead, great Cyrus and Alexander, how near you both seem to me; do I dream? or are they really there? I pinch myself to find out if I am awake, yes, there on the table by my side are two coins which I dug up in my vineyard last year, with the profiles of bearded Commodus dressed as Hercules, and Crispina Augusta, with her heavy chin and her shrewish nose. — "This is no dream," say I; "for here is Rome between my thumb and forefinger."

My greatest pleasure was to lose myself in reflections on moral issues; to raise once more, questions long settled by force; should I cross the Rubicon, — or not? I could never make up my mind! I fought Brutus and Cæsar in turn; changed my opinion and argued on either side with so much eloquence that I could not tell what I believed. In this way the subject takes possession of you, as you give and take, strike out and hit back, till at last you are transfixed by your own blade! Did you ever hear of such an idea? But it all comes of reading Plutarch, with his smooth tongue, and pleasant way of calling you "my friend"! He gets you first on one side and then on the other; and has as many points of view as he has stories to tell you; so that the hero I love best is always the last one that I have read about.

We are all chained to Fortune's car; her triumphs over history are greater than Pompey's, as her wheel turns, never resting for a moment. She has as many phases as the moon, says Menelaus, in the words Sophocles puts into his mouth; and for those who are still in her first quarter, that is a comforting reflection.

I would sometimes say to myself: "What does all this matter, Breugnon? What to you are the glories of Rome, and the crimes and follies of these old rascals? You have your own faults and troubles to think of, why go out of your way to worry over those of people who have been dead and gone for eighteen hundred years? To a sober middle-class citizen of Clamecy, Cæsar, Antony, and their light-o'-love, Cleopatra, these Persian princes who murdered their sons and married their daughters, were extremely depraved people; the most virtuous thing they ever did was to die; so peace to their ashes!—but how can a respectable man find pleasure in reading about such insanities? Think of Alexander, who spent the treasures of a nation on the burial of his beautiful favorite, Ephestion. Are you not shocked by such extravagance?—It is bad enough to murder a lot of people, for men are savage beasts; but when it comes to wasting so much good money, that these tyrants had never earned, how can you smile at such wickedness? It is really absurd to see you sitting up with your eyes wide open, as proud as if you yourself had been fool enough to scatter these millions to the wind. Surely the worst idiot of all is he who delights in the follies of others!"

After a discourse of this kind, the other side of me would make answer: "Colas, you talk like a printed book, but, none the less, I would give my right hand for these things which you call nonsense; and I find more life in the shadows of the men who died two thousand years ago, than in those who move and breathe today. I feel that I know and love them, and would consent to let Alexander kill me as he did Clytus, if afterward he would come and weep over my body. It is all real to me; my heart is in my throat when I see Caesar in the Senate-house, his back against a pillar like a stag at bay, the conspirators' knives searching for his life; and I am in ecstasy when Cleopatra floats by me in her gilded barge, surrounded by Nereids and young pages, naked and beautiful as the day. The perfumed breeze blows across my face, and I open my big nostrils, the better to inhale the delicious fragrance."

When at the end Antony is drawn up to the loophole in the tower, bleeding, half dead; and his love, struggling with the heavy weight, can hardly pull him in;—I really cannot bear it, and sob like a child! What is it that moves me thus, and binds me to these men and women as if to those of my own blood? except the fact that we are truly of one family, we are Man, each and all of us.

I pity people from the bottom of my heart who know nothing of the profound pleasure of books; they are like disinherited children, but they do not know it, and boast that the present is enough for them. Blind geese! who can see no farther than the end of their noses! Not that I mean to deny the merits of the present; that would come with an ill grace from one like me, who have always kept my hands and my mouth open for anything good. No, those who find fault with the present are ignorant, or else they have a poor digestion: I understand a man who clasps all that he can reach to his heart, but there are those who reach nothing worth while:—he who contents himself with little is of small value; and I have always preferred to take the most that I could get in life.

In Adam's time the present was all very well; there were no clothes to wear, and only one woman in the world; but life is fuller now, coming as we do at the end of a long line of ancestors, heirs to all that they have amassed, and we should be fools indeed to neglect the harvests of the past, on the pretext that we can gather others.

I often dwell on the thought of Adam. He and I are really the same person, only I am older and bigger; the same tree, but with more branches. I feel every stroke of the woodman's axe to my remotest leaf; all the joys and sorrows of the world are mine; I laugh with them that rejoice, and weep with them that weep; and this is especially true of the world of books; there, more than in my own life, I feel the bond that unites men, from prince to peasant.

Soon of us all there will remain only a few ashes, and the flame which rises, one yet infinitely multiplied, from our inmost souls towards Heaven. There with its thousand tongues it will sing forever the glory of the Omnipotent Creator.

So I lie dreaming in my garret, while outside the wind falls with the fading light, and the chill wings of the snow brush across the window panes. As the shadows darken my eyes can no longer distinguish the book in my hand, but with my face on the page the human scent comes to my nostrils; is it I, or the story that is dying away into the night, that comes, that is here? I am in the forest, my prey eludes me in the long vistas, as I seem to stop and listen with a beating heart to the flight and the pursuit: my eyes slowly close, but they can pierce through the darkness; I am not asleep, the planets are looking at me through the window, I can almost touch the glass, and across the black arch without flashes one shooting star, then another,—a rain of jewels this November night; and I think of Cæsar and his comet,—perhaps that is the trail of his blood up yonder!

At dawn I am still there dreaming. It is Sunday; I hear the church bells, and their sound fills the whole house from cellar to garret with its vibrations, giving new life to my vagrant fancies, which spread themselves over poor old Paillard's book. To my ear my dim little chamber resounds to the feet of armies, the wheels of chariots, and the tramp of war-steeds. The windows shake, my ears and my heart thrill with the sound, and I open my mouth to cry: "Ave Cæsar Imperator!"—when Florimond, who has come up and is looking out of the window, says with a loud yawn: "There is not a single soul to be seen in the street this morning,—it is as dull as ditch-water!"

XIV
Health to the King!

THE air was delightfully soft and warm when I woke this morning; it seemed like a gentle touch on my cheek, or a kitten rubbing itself against me. It flowed in a golden stream through the window; the sky had raised her cloudy eyelids, and looked at me with her pale blue eyes, while a faint ray of sunshine smiled from the opposite roof.

I felt dreamy and languid and like a boy again, — old fool that I am! But I have stopped growing old and am now retracing my steps as fast as I can; pretty soon I shall be an infant in arms once more. My heart was filled with sweet visions, — like good Roger who yearned for Alcine, — you remember? I was in such a tender humor that I could not have been persuaded to harm a fly, and any child could have played with me.

I thought I was alone, but all at once I caught sight of Martine in the corner; I had not noticed when she came in, for she had said nothing, contrary to her habit, but just sat down and took up her sewing without even looking in my direction. I felt on such good terms with all the world that I wanted to share my pleasure, so just for the sake of being amiable, I said, "Why did they ring the great bell this morning?"

"It is St. Martin's Day, Father," said she, surprised at the question.

To think that I should have so lost myself in dreams as to forget the god of our town and herself! Among all the new friends in Plutarch, I could see in my mind's eye this old one, as good as any of the rest of them, dividing his long cloak with his sword, as his legend tells us. "How could I forget St. Martin?" cried I.

"I don't know indeed," said Martine, "except that these days you don't seem to remember anything in earth or Heaven but that stupid book of yours."

This made me laugh, for I had often noticed that she cast a malevolent eye on old Plutarch when she came in the morning and found him in my bed; women seldom have a real love for books; they see in them either lovers or rivals. When they themselves read they always have an uneasy sense of infidelity, and that is why they cannot bear to see us absorbed in books, which they feel to be a sort of treachery.

"It is St. Martin's own fault," said I, "he never comes to see me nowadays, though he has half his cloak to wear, and so I forgot all about him. Out of sight out of mind! You must keep yourself before people's eyes, you know, my daughter, if you want to be remembered."

"There is no need to tell me that; I don't let folks forget me."

"True enough, you are easy to see and hear as a general thing, but this morning you were as still as a mouse; I miss our usual quarrel, come over here and begin."

She would not even turn her head, but answered, "I have given up, there is no use talking to you!"

I looked at her as she sat stitching away with her mouth obstinately set; she really looked sad, so I began to be sorry that I had got the better of her. "Come here, dear, and give me a kiss; I may forget Martin, but never his namesake. Come, I have a present here for you."

"You have some trick up your sleeve."

"No, no, on my word, come and see what I have for you."

"I am too busy."

"Unnatural child, you are too busy to kiss your old father?"

She came reluctantly and stood near the bed, and I held out my arms to her.

"I don't see any present," said she.

"You have it now, I meant myself."

"A pretty present you would be!"

"Ugly or pretty, I am yours entirely now to do with as you please."

"Will you sleep downstairs?"

"Anywhere you choose to put me."

"Will you do as you are told and let me love you and scold you when you need it?"

"I am your slave from this hour!"

"You dear bad old thing!" she cried. "I am going to get even with you now, for all your obstinacy!"

Then she hugged and cuffed me, shaking me about like a doll, and, without waiting a minute, called Florimond and his white-capped assistants who carried me feet first down the narrow stair and put me down in the big bed in the bright room, and there Martine and Glodie tucked me up and fussed about me, telling me over and over again that now that they had me downstairs I should see what good care they would take of me.

Do you know I really enjoyed it? And, having given in to my daughter completely, strangely enough I find that it is I who really direct and manage the whole household.

Martine spends the greater part of the day in my room now and we have long talks about one time in particular when *I* sat by *her* bedside, because it was she who was laid up with a sprained foot. The naughty little cat had jumped out of the window one night to meet her sweetheart; I caught her, and in spite of the sprain, I gave her a good trouncing; she laughs at it now and says I did not hurt enough, but in those days it was impossible to keep her in order no matter what you did; she always managed to slip through my fingers, but she kept her head nevertheless and some one else lost his, we must suppose, as he is now her husband. She laughs and sighs over those old days, and says it is all over now; that there are no more jokes for her; and then we talk of Florimond. She does justice to his good qualities, like the sensible woman that she is, but admits that he does not amuse her; marriage, however, is not intended for an amusement.

"No one knows that better than you do, Father, but we must make the best of what we have. You might as well try to draw water out of a sieve as to look for love in a husband, but I am not one to cry my eyes out for what I cannot have; I am not so badly off, and contented enough on the whole; but I can't help thinking how different things are now from what I used to expect. How far our youthful dreams are from the things we come to accept in later years! I don't know if it is sad or ridiculous, but when I remember all the hopes and fears, vows and flames, and for what? To make some man's pot boil. After all, it is as much as most of us deserve, but if any one had told me so, once upon a time! — Well, there is always some fun to be got out of it. Laughter is a sauce that would make anything taste good, and that has never been lacking to you and me, Daddy; we can always laugh when we have made fools of ourselves."

Such as it was, you can be sure we did not deny ourselves that consolation, and had many a joke, too, at the expense of other people. Sometimes we would fall silent; she occupied with her work and I with my book; but we kept up a little murmur like a brook which flows underground till it can leap out again into the sunshine; an idea would come into Martine's head which made her burst out laughing, and then our tongues would run on again faster than ever.

I should have been glad to introduce Plutarch to Martine, and make her appreciate all his beauties, and enjoy my interesting and pathetic manner of reading aloud, but I had no sort of success; she did not like Greece or Rome any more than a fish would like apples for his dinner. Sometimes she would listen for a few moments, just from politeness, but she could not keep her mind on it, or rather her thoughts were elsewhere, flying up, down and all around, so that at the most exciting part of the narrative when I was working up to my effect, with a trembling voice, she would interrupt me, calling out to Glodie, or to Florimond at the other end of the house. This vexed me, of course, but I had to give it up, and resign myself to the fact that woman rarely shares our visions with us. She is half of us, but which half? The upper, of course, but suppose it should be the other? One thing is very sure, whatever the sexes have in common, it is not their brain, for each has its own, like a case full of baubles; or rather, they are like two sprouts from the same stem with one root between them—the heart.

I have a great many visitors these days, old graybeard as I am, ruined and lame into the bargain; all the pretty young housewives of the neighborhood gather round my bed, ostensibly to bring me the news, or to ask to have something mended.

It does not matter what excuse they make for coming, they forget all about it as soon as they are inside the door; it is like the market, where each one has her place; Guillemine the bright-eyed, Huguette with her straight nose, clever Jacquotte, Margueron, Alizon, and all the rest of them, and the old man in the middle, snug under his down comforter. Such gossiping and such a clack of tongues, with their gay laughter ringing out like bells—mine is the big deep one. I know a lot of good stories which hit the girls in the right spot, and they laugh sometimes till they roll on the floor, and you can hear them across the street.

Florimond was actually jealous of my popularity, and wanted me to tell him the secret of my success. I said that it was an open secret; I was young, that was all; but he said rather spitefully that he knew that it was because I had such a bad reputation, as women always like a rake.

"True enough," said I, "you know how boys admire an old soldier, when he comes back from the field of glory, and in the same way the ladies like Colas because they understand each other; they think he has fought in the campaigns of Love, and may perhaps live to fight another day."

"Did any one ever hear such an old wretch?" cried Martine, "to be talking of making love at his time of life!"

"Why not? Now that you have put the idea into my head, I have a great mind to marry again."

"Much good may it do you! But, after all, boys will be boys!"

December 6th,
St. Nicholas Day.
I got out of bed this morning to do honor to the anniversary, and they rolled my great armchair between the table and the window, set a foot-warmer under my feet, and placed a little desk before me, with a socket for the candle.

About ten o'clock appeared the brotherhood of sailors, boat-builders, and workmen on the river. First came their players and the banner, and then they all passed by our windows arm in arm, dancing and singing, on their way to church, perhaps to the wineshop later. They saw me and stopped to cheer, so I stood up, and my patron saint and I exchanged salutations. Then I leaned down and shook as many of their black paws as I could reach, and poured a drop or two into each of the big mouths, though it was like trying to sprinkle a field.

My four sons came at twelve o'clock to offer me the compliments of the season, for no matter on what terms one lives for the rest of the year, a father's name-day is sacred; the whole family life revolves around it as on a pivot; it is a bond which draws us all together, and I attach a great deal of importance to it. I don't know that the four enjoyed themselves much when they were all there together, for in fact I am the only real tie between them, as they have but little love for each other.

It is a sign of our times, this relaxation of those ties between men, the home, family, and religion; each trusts in his own wisdom now, and wants to live for himself alone. I am not one of those old men who are always grumbling and complaining of the present day, and predicting disaster; I know that the world will outlast my time, and that the young know their own business as well as ever their fathers did. Yes, but the old have a hard part to play where all around them is change and renewal; they must alter too or there is no room for them, and that is precisely what I do not want to do. I prefer to sit here in my chair just as I am; the only thing I am willing to change is my mind, and only that when it is absolutely necessary. I can turn my ideas inside out, but they are the same thing after all, and meanwhile I can look on at the shifting scenes and the young people whom I admire, but none the less I lie in wait for the chance to guide them in the way I would have them go.

When we all gathered round the dinner table I had at my right hand John Francis, who is a bigoted Catholic; on my left, my son Anthony from Lyons, who is an equally bigoted Huguenot. They sat up stiffly on their chairs, staring straight before them, so as not to be obliged to look at one another.

John Francis is a smiling prosperous man with a hard shrewd eye; he talked interminably of his business, boasted of his money and of the fine linen that he sold by the special favor of Providence. Anthony's lips are shaved but he wears a little beard on his chin; and is morose and cold in his manner. He also talked of his trade in books, his journeys to Geneva, his affairs generally, and attributed his prosperity to God, but it seemed to be a different Deity. Neither listened, but kept on monotonously repeating the same refrain, until at last they became annoyed and began to introduce topics of a controversial nature, one dwelling on the progress of *The* Religion, the other on the stability of *The* True Faith; all the time each ignored his antagonist, sat as if nailed to his seat, and spoke with the utmost contempt, and in a sharp rasping voice, of the enemies' God.

In the middle of the table sat my son Michael, sergeant in the Sacermore regiment; he is called a rascal, but is not a bad fellow on the whole, and the behavior of his brothers diverted him extremely, sending him into fits of laughter. He kept turning from one to the other, like an animal in a cage, to stare into the angry faces of his elders, and at last interrupted them without ceremony, telling them that they were fat sheep of the same breed even if their fleece was marked with a different brand, and that he had seen plenty of their sort killed and eaten.

The youngest son Anisse sat and gazed at him with horror. His name was certainly well chosen, for he never could have invented gunpowder; discussions are his abhorrence, for he takes no real interest in anything on earth; his only joy is to yawn and dawdle throughout the livelong day. Politics and religion seem to him diabolical inventions to disturb the sleep of sensible men. "Good or bad," he would say, "what I have is enough for me, so why change it? Why turn over the mattress when I made the hole in the middle myself?" Poor fellow! people will persist in shaking up his feather-bed whether he likes it or not, which angers him so much that, mild as he is, he would like to send his disturbers to instant execution. His brothers' loud voices positively scared him, making him duck his head as if to avoid a blow.

I was all eyes and ears as I sat there taking them in, and it amused me to unravel the part of myself that was in each of my four sons, for mine they are beyond a doubt. If something in them came out of me, it must have gone into me at one time or another, but I do not find anywhere in my skin a trace of the preacher, the priest, or the sheep. (Perhaps I might discover the adventurer if I looked closely.) But the germs must have been there, and Nature has betrayed me. Yes, I can recognize my own gestures and ways of speaking, even of thinking. I can see myself in these men, but disguised, and that is what is rather confusing; but underneath it is the very same person, one and various. We each contain many personalities, good, bad and indifferent, the wolf, the lamb, the watch-dog, the honest man and the scamp, but one of the number is sure to be the strongest, and dominates all the rest, who escape as soon as they can by the first open door.

I am filled with self-reproach when I see these escaped sons of mine, so remote, yet so near to me. My little boys they must always be too, and even when they are most foolish, I feel that I ought to apologize to them, for is it not all my fault? Luckily enough they are perfectly contented and satisfied with themselves, and that is as it should be, but their intolerance is what I cannot bear. Why cannot they live, and let others live, in peace? There they were, all four, like so many fighting-cocks, ready to peck and jump at each other, but by this time I had had enough of it, and observed placidly, "Well, my lambs, I see that it would not be easy to pull the wool from your backs, and I am proud to see you show your good blood,—mine, I mean,—and make yourselves heard, but now be still, all of you, and let me have a chance to talk, for I have something I have been dying to say for the last half hour."

Far from obeying me on the instant, some chance word excited them so that they broke into a perfect storm of rage; John Francis caught up a chair, Michael drew his long sword, and Anthony a dagger, while Anisse employed his only weapon by bleating, "Murder! Fire!" in a lamentable voice.

Upon my honor I was afraid that they would cut each other's throats, but I seized the first thing that came to my hand (unluckily it was the ewer with the doves, pride of Florimond's heart), and dashed it in fragments on the table. The noise checked the combatants, and at the same moment, Martine ran in with a pot of boiling water and threatened to sprinkle it over them if they did not stop fighting. They still clamored and disputed, but when I raise my voice, other donkeys have to cease braying.

"I am master here," I cried, "and I tell you I will have no more of this. Shut up! Are you all crazy, or do you take this for the Council of Nicea? If you want subjects to discuss, pick out something of our own day, for I am bored to death with your old quarrels. If the doctor has ordered you to dispute by way of exercise, you can wrangle over the merits of these wines, the food on the table, or anything you can see or touch, and then there will be some way to decide the controversy; but to differ about the Holy Ghost, or the mind of God, is as much as to say that you have no minds of your own. I am not opposed to faith; I believe, he believes, you believe, as much as you please, but don't let us talk so much about it. There are plenty of other interesting topics in the world, and, since each of you is perfectly sure to go to Heaven, with a place reserved for you, and all the people who differ from you barred out, let us be happy meanwhile, and leave the good Lord to arrange His household as seems good to Him. Surely He is able to look after His own affairs without assistance from us; He reigns in Heaven, and we on earth; our business is to make it as habitable a place as possible, and to that end we must all do our share; not one of us can be spared; even you four can be useful in your day and generation. Your country needs your faith, John Francis, as much as yours, Anthony; Michael's adventurous spirit and Anisse's stay-at-home qualities are equally valuable; for you are the four pillars of the house, and if one gives way, the whole building falls to the ground, and will overwhelm you all in ruin. Surely you must be convinced by such masterly reasoning, and will agree that you do not wish anything so unnecessary. What would you think of sailors in a storm at sea if they fell to disputing instead of taking in sail?

"I will tell you a story about King Henry and our late Duke. They were lamenting the warlike disposition of the French nation which led to perpetual civil wars. 'Ventresaintgris!' exclaimed the King, 'but I should like to take these furious monks and preachers of the Gospel, sew them up in a sack like a litter of cats, and throw them into the Loire!' The Duke replied that he had heard there was an island where the rulers of Berne sent quarrelsome husbands and wives; when a boat returned for them a month later, it found the couple cooing like a pair of turtle doves. ' I should like to tie our rival religionists up in bundles and pack them off to that isle, hoping for the same result,' concluded his lordship, laughing.

"Now, my children," said I, "you need the same kind of treatment. Why do you grunt and turn your backs on each other? Each of you may think himself of finer clay than his brothers, but the fact is you are all

Breugnons, chips of the old block, thorough-bred Burgundians. You all have big crooked noses, and wide mouths like wine-funnels; your eyes look out fiercely from under bushy eyebrows, but there is a twinkle in them all the same. The artist's signature is plain to see on the four of you, so can't you understand that if you hurt your brothers, you are injuring yourself as well? That it is for your own interest to be united? What if you don't think alike on some questions? That is rather an advantage than otherwise, for you cannot all plow the same field; on the contrary, the more fields and opinions there are in the family, the greater our strength and happiness. Reach out then into the world as far as you possibly can, and increase your portion of land and thought. Each for himself and all for each, and may the long Breugnon nose point the way to the future glory of the family! Come, boys, shake hands and be friends!"

For a moment they still looked sulkily at each other, but I could see the clouds parting, and all at once Michael flung his arms round John Francis, with a loud laugh, "Embrace me, Brother-Big-Nose!" cried he, and the others followed his example.

"Come, Martine, let us drink to the Breugnon brothers ourselves!!"

A few moments before, when I broke the ewer in my anger, I had cut my wrist a little, and left a little blood on the table. Anthony held his glass under the scratch in his pompous manner, and caught a drop.

"Let this wine from our father's veins be the seal of our reconciliation."

"What a disgusting idea!" I cried; "to think of spoiling good wine with such a mixture! Throw it away, and if you want to drink my blood, you'll find it in a bottle of the best!"and thereupon we all drank and all agreed as to the vintage.

When they had gone and Martine was binding up my wrist, she said slyly, "You succeeded at last, you old scamp, didn't you?"

"Succeeded in what? In stopping the quarrel?"

"You know well enough what I mean," and she pointed to the broken fragments of the ewer on the table.

I pretended not to understand, and, with the most innocent expression, declared that I had not the least idea what she meant, but I could not help laughing, and she boxed my ears for an old rascal.

"I couldn't stand the sight of it another minute," I said, "it was really too hideous; either that ewer or I had to perish!"

"The one that remains is none too handsome."

"That does not trouble me, you know, for I don't have to look at him."

Christmas Eve.

Now as the winter draws on the shortening days are like precious stuffs folded away into the coffer of the nights, only to reappear, already growing longer, on St. Lucy's Day. The seasons have turned once more on their well-oiled hinges, the door has shut and opened again, and through the crack the new year begins to shine.

As I sit this Christmas Eve under the great chimney-hood, I am as it were at the bottom of a well, and can look up and see the bright stars winking in the sky, and from far off comes the sound of the bells ringing for midnight mass. I love to think that the Child was born at this dead hour when all the world was still. His voice speaks to us of the coming day and of the New Year, and Hope, with her warm wings, broods over the frozen night and softens it.

My children have all gone to church, but I have missed it for the first time in my life, and I am here alone with my dog Citron, and the household cat Patapon. A little while ago we were all gathered round the hearth, and I was telling Glodie wonderful fairy tales. You should see her open her round eyes at the story of Bout-de-Canard and the little bald chicken, or of the boy who made a fortune out of his cock by selling it to people who wanted to know when the day was coming, so that they could carry it away in their carts. It was too amusing to see her, and the others listening and laughing, every one putting in his word.

Sometimes when we were silent for a minute we could hear the water bubbling in the kettle, a log falling in the fire, the cricket's shrill voice, and, outside, the wind sweeping against the window. I love these snug winter evenings, the silence, the sense of intimacy, when my fancies can wander far afield and return safe to the home nest.

I have been making up my budget for the last year, and I find that in six months I have lost all that I possessed; my wife, my house, my money, and my legs; and yet, absurd as it sounds to say so, on striking a balance, I find myself as rich as ever. How can that be, when I have nothing?

No burdens, would be nearer the truth; for I find myself lightened of care, happier, freer than the wind that blows; I would not have believed it, if, last year, any one had predicted what would happen and that I should take it in this spirit; I had always sworn that whatever came, to the day of my death, I would be master in my own house, independent, owing nothing to any one but myself. Well, we do not know what a day will bring forth. Things turn out so differently from what we intended, and we are nevertheless content.

Man is a wonderful creature and all is grist that comes to his mill. Happiness, suffering, feast or famine, he can adjust himself to any of them. He can go on four legs or on one; he may be deaf, dumb or blind, he will still manage to get along, and see, hear and speak in the depths of his own soul. Everything is shaped and formed by that soul of his, and how delightful it is to have such a mind and body! To feel that if need be one can swim like a fish, fly like a bird, bathe in fire like a salamander, or wrestle successfully with all four elements as man does on the ground. In this way we gain through our losses, for our minds can supply what has been taken away, so that the less we have the more we are, as a pruned tree grows stronger and more beautiful.

The clock strikes midnight.

Hark to the Christmas hymn, "Unto us a Child is born."

Epiphany.

It really is a joke how I keep on adding to my possessions now that I have nothing at all, and the secret is that I have learned to enjoy the riches of others, and so have none of the drawbacks.

I have read horrid stories of poor old fathers who stripped themselves of all their goods for their children's sake, and then found themselves neglected and forlorn, conscious that their wicked offspring already wished them dead and buried. I can only say that these unfortunate old men must have mismanaged the whole thing, and, for my part, I have never been so well looked after, so much loved and petted as I am now in my poverty.

I kept some things from my prosperous days which are better than gold and silver. I have my good spirits still, and lots more treasures that I picked up in the course of my life; gaiety and sharpness, wisdom and folly. I have enough for all comers, so if my children give me a good deal, they get something back, and if the account does not balance evenly, we throw in affection for good measure.

If you would like to see an uncrowned King, a landless but happy man, look at Breugnon as he sits throned tonight at the merry feast of the Epiphany. There was a great procession in the afternoon which went by our windows; the three Magi with their attendants, a chorus of shepherds and shepherdesses, and all the dogs in the town; now in the evening we are all gathered round the table, thirty of us, including me, children, and grandchildren; and they all drank my health together, crying, "Here's to the King!" for they have crowned me with a splendid paper crown, and Martine is my queen; (you see, like those old fellows in Plutarch, I have married my daughter) so whenever I carry my glass to my lips, every one applauds; and then I laugh and the wine goes down the wrong way. My queen not only shares my drink herself, but there is another person who shares too in his own way, and that is my youngest grandson, who lies in his mother's arms, red and squalling. Every one is happy down to the dog and cat picking up bones under the table.

I hate to keep my thoughts to myself, so I say aloud:

"The only fault I have to find with this good life of ours, my friends, is that it is too short. I don't feel as if I had had my money's worth, and though I may be told that I ought to be satisfied with what has fallen to my lot, I can only say that I should like to have more, a second slice of cake, if I could get it without making too much fuss. And then it makes me unhappy to think of all the good fellows who are gone. Of what use is it to be here alone? Ah, how Time flows on, and with it good men like King Henry and our Duke Louis!"

The thought of them was enough to set me off, on former times and recollections, and I told old stories till, I am sorry to say, I grew tired and began to repeat myself; but my children did not mind, and when I became confused and forgot anything, they would fill up the gap; and then I would pull myself together and find them all laughing.

"Well, Father, those were great days when you were young! What figures the women must have had, and what splendid fellows the men were! As for King Henry and his friend the Duke, they have not their equal nowadays!"

"All right," I reply, "laugh and grow fat. I know there is still good fish in the sea, and good men to catch it, and for one that goes, three will come after. There will never be a lack of good stout sons of Gaul, but my trouble is that they will not be the same ones that I knew and loved, like King Henry who is gone; but never mind, Colas, there is nothing to cry about. I should think not indeed! for you surely don't want to keep on chewing the same cud for ever. The wine is just as good even if it is not out of the old casks, and here's to the King and his people!

"Frankly, dear children, I love myself better than any King, so liberty for us, my countrymen! and to the devil with our rulers! As long as we are here, the land I love, and I, all is well; so what need have we of a King on earth or in Heaven? Or of a throne for him to sit on? Let each man have his share of the sun and shade, his bit of land, and his arms to work with, no one could ask more; and if the King in person came to my house I would say, 'Come in and sit down, for we are all equal together in France, each master in his own kingdom, and here's to your good health, my guest and cousin.'"

"How is this?" said Brother John, "art thou also a poet? — By the help of God, I can string rhymes together as well as another; I am sure of it; have but patience with me if my verses should prove of the wrong color—"

— *PANTAGRUEL, V. 46.*

Books published by Mondial

French Classics:

1. Rougon-Macquart Series:

Emile Zola: The Fortune of the Rougons
ISBN 1595690107 / 9781595690104

Emile Zola: The Fat and the Thin (The Belly of Paris)
ISBN 1595690522 / 9781595690524

Emile Zola: Abbe Mouret's Transgression
(The Sin of the Abbé Mouret) ISBN 1595690506 / 9781595690500

Emile Zola: The Dream. ISBN 1595690492 / 9781595690494

Emile Zola: A Love Episode (A Page of Love)
ISBN 1595690271 / 9781595690272

Emile Zola: The Conquest of Plassans
ISBN 1595690484 / 9781595690487

Emile Zola: The Joy of Life (Zest for Life)
ISBN 1595690476 / ISBN 9781595690470

Emile Zola: Doctor Pascal. ISBN 1595690514 / 9781595690517

Emile Zola: His Excellency (His Excellency, Eugène Rougon)
ISBN 1595690557 / 9781595690555

Emile Zola: Money. ISBN 9781595690630

Emile Zola: Piping Hot! (Pot Bouille). *Illustrated Edition.*
ISBN 9781595691231

Emile Zola: The Soil (The Earth). ISBN 9781595690883

Emile Zola: The Downfall (La Debacle). ISBN 9781595691118

2. Other French Literature:

Emile Zola: The Mysteries of Marseille. ISBN 9781595690913

Emile Zola: The Flood. ISBN 9781595690944

Emile Zola: Death. ISBN 9781595690937

Emile Zola: Fruitfulness ISBN 1595690182 / 9781595690180

Emile Zola: For a Night of Love. ISBN 9781595691217

Emile Zola: The Fête in Coqueville
(The Coqueville Spree) ISBN 9781595690869

Emile Zola: Jean Gourdon's Four Days. ISBN 9781595691224

Victor Hugo: Ninety-Three. ISBN 9781595690920

Victor Hugo: Bug-Jargal. ISBN 9781595690951

Victor Hugo: The Man Who Laughs (By Order of the King)
ISBN 1595690131 / 9781595690135

Victor Hugo: History of a Crime. ISBN 1595690204 / 9781595690203

Voltaire: The Princess of Babylon. ISBN 9781595690999

Honoré de Balzac: Ursula (Ursule Mirouet). ISBN 9781595690531

Honoré de Balzac: Maitre Cornelius. ISBN 9781595690173

Anatole France: Penguin Island. ISBN 1595690298 / 9781595690296

Anatole France: The Crime of Sylvestre Bonnard
ISBN 9781595690593

Anatole France: The Gods are Athirst (Les Dieux ont soif)
ISBN 9781595690128

Gustave Flaubert: Salammbo (Salambo) ISBN 1595690352 / 9781595690357

Romain Rolland: Pierre and Luce . ISBN 9781595690609

Romain Rolland: Colas Breugnon. A Burgundian Story.
ISBN 9781595691330

Jules Verne: An Antarctic Mystery (The Sphinx of the Ice Fields)
ISBN 1595690549 / 9781595690548

André Gide: Strait is the Gate. (La Porte étroite) ISBN 9781595690623

André Gide: Prometheus Illbound. ISBN 9781595690807

André Gide: Recollections of Oscar Wilde. ISBN 9781595690814

Alphonse Daudet:
Little What's-His-Name (aka Little Good-for-Nothing)
(Le Petit Chose. French Classics) ISBN 9781595691057

German Classics:

Heinrich Heine: Germany. A Winter Tale (Deutschland. Ein
Wintermärchen.) Bilingual Edition. ISBN 9781595690715

Heinrich Heine: The Rabbi of Bacharach
(German Classics) ISBN 9781595691002

Heinrich Heine: Florentine Nights.
(German Classics) ISBN 9781595691019

Heinrich Heine: From the Memoirs of Herr von Schnabelewopski
(German Classics) ISBN 9781595691026

Theodor Fontane: Trials and Tribulations. A Berlin Novel
(German Classics) ISBN 9781595691255

Bernhard Kellermann: God's Beloved (Illustrated)
(German Classics) ISBN 9781595691262

Gotthold Ephraim Lessing: Minna von Barnhelm or The Soldier's Fortune
(German Classics) . ISBN: 9781595691248

Johann Wolfgang von Goethe: The Sorrows of Young Werther
ISBN 159569045X / 9781595690456

Theodor Storm: The Rider of the White Horse
(The Dikegrave; aka The Dykemaster) ISBN 9781595690746

Heinrich von Kleist: Michael Kohlhaas
(A Tale from an Old Chronicle) ISBN 9781595690760

Gottfried Keller: A Village Romeo and Juliet
(Swiss-German Classics) ISBN 9781595690791

Gottfried Keller: Ursula (Swiss-German Classics). ISBN 9781595690838

Gottfried Keller: The Governor of Greifensee
(Swiss-German Classics) ISBN 9781595690845

Wilhelm Raabe: The Hunger Pastor
(German Classics) ISBN 9781595690753

Theodor Storm, Adelbert von Chamisso, Adalbert Stifter: Famous German Novellas of the 19th Century (Immensee. Peter Schlemihl. Brigitta.) ISBN 159569014X / 9781595690142

Franz Grillparzer: The Poor Musician. (Austrian Classics) ISBN 9781595691095

Marie von Ebner-Eschenbach: Krambambuli. The District Doctor (Two Novellas. Austrian Classics). ISBN 9781595691040

E. T. A. Hoffmann: The Sandman. The Elementary Spirit (Two Tales. German Classics). ISBN 9781595691170

Wilhelm Hauff: The Cold Heart. Nose, the Dwarf (Two Tales. German Classics). ISBN 9781595691187

Danish Classics:

Martin Andersen Nexo: Pelle the Conqueror (Complete Edition: Boyhood. Apprenticeship. The Great Struggle. Daybreak.) ISBN 159569028X / 9781595690289

Martin Andersen Nexo: Ditte Everywoman (Complete Edition: Girl Alive. Daughter of Man. Towards the Stars.) ISBN 9781595690333

Italian Classics:

Gabriele D'Annunzio: The Child of Pleasure. ISBN 9781595690581

Luigi Pirandello: Signora Speranza. ISBN 9781595691088:

African Literature:

Malama Katulwende: Bitterness (An African Novel from Zambia) ISBN 159569031X / 9781595690319

British Classics:

Oscar Wilde: The Critic as Artist. Upon the Importance of Doing Nothing and Discussing Everything. ISBN 9781595690821

H. G. Wells: Tales of Space and Time. ISBN 9781595691220

Rudyard Kipling: Ghost Stories. ISBN 9781595691323

Oscar Wilde, Anonymous: Teleny or The Reverse of the Medal
(Gay erotic classic) ISBN 1595690360 / 9781595690364

Agatha Christie: Two Novels (The Mysterious Affair at Styles.
The Secret Adversary.) ISBN 1595690417 / 9781595690418

Jerome K. Jerome: Idle Thoughts of an Idle Fellow
ISBN 1595690247 / 9781595690241

Virgina Woolf: Jacob's Room. ISBN 9781595691149

Jane Austen: Persuasion. Northanger Abbey (Two Novels)
ISBN: 9781595691156

William Somerset Maugham: The Trembling of a Leaf
ISBN 9781595691194

Howard Overing Sturgis: Belchamber. ISBN 9781595691316

Howard Overing Sturgis: All That Was possible. ISBN 9781595691293

Howard Overing Sturgis: Tim. ISBN 9781595691309

US-American Literature:

Jack London: War of the Classes. Revolution. The Shrinkage of the Planet.
ISBN 1595690409 / 9781595690401

Jack London: Before Adam. Children of the Frost.
ISBN 1595690395 / 9781595690395

Jack London: The Iron Heel. ISBN 1595690379 / 9781595690371

Jack London: Burning Daylight. ISBN 9781595691064

Donald Windham: Two People (Gay Classics). ISBN 9781595691033

Susan Coolidge: Clover. ISBN 1595690263 / 9781595690265

Gertrude Stein: Three Lives (With an Introduction by Carl Van Vechten).
ISBN 1595690425 / 9781595690425

Sinclair Lewis: The Trail of the Hawk. ISBN 9781595691132

Carl Van Vechten: Firecrackers. A Realistic Novel. ISBN 9781595690685

Bruce Kellner: Winter Ridge (A Love Story) ISBN 9781595690692

Polish Classics:

Adam Mickiewicz: Pan Tadeusz or The Last Foray in Lithuania (aka Pan Thaddeus / Mister Thaddeus). ISBN 9781595691347

Gay Classics:

Oscar Wilde, Anonymous: Teleny or The Reverse of the Medal (Gay erotic classic) ISBN 1595690360 / 9781595690364

Donald Windham: Two People (Gay Classics). ISBN 9781595691033

Howard Overing Sturgis: Tim. ISBN 9781595691309

Contemporary Literature:

Bruce Kellner: Winter Ridge. A Love Story. ISBN 9781595690692

Malama Katulwende: Bitterness (An African Novel from Zambia) ISBN 159569031X / 9781595690319

Other Books:

Frederick (Friedrich) Engels: Socialism: Utopian and Scientific (Appendix: The Mark; Preface by Karl Marx) ISBN 1595690468 / 9781595690463

Karl Marx: The Eighteenth Brumaire of Louis Bonaparte. ISBN 1595690239 / 9781595690234

Frederick (Friedrich) Engels: Feuerbach — The Roots of the Socialist Philosophy. **Karl Marx:** Theses on Feuerbach ISBN 9781595691286

Sigmund Freud: Dream Psychology (Psychoanalysis for Beginners) ISBN 9781595690166

www.ingramcontent.com/pod-product-compliance
Lightning Source LLC
Chambersburg PA
CBHW030519260626
47157CB00005B/1807